I0618666

THE ROUGH OLD STUFF

FROM

MIKE SHAYNE MYSTERY MAGAZINE

By Dick Stodghill

JLT-CHARATAN PUBLICATIONS

Copyright 2007 by Dick Stodghill.

All rights reserved. No part of this book may be reproduced, stored in a retrieval system or transmitted in any form or by any means without prior written permission of the author, except by a reviewer who may quote brief passages in a review to be printed in a newspaper, magazine or journal.

First Printing

ISBN: 978-0-6151-5364-3
JLT-Charatan Publications

Dedicated to the fine memories of Black Mask, Dime Detective, Mike Shayne, Manhunt, Espionage, The Saint and all the other great magazines that in years long past closed the cover on their final edition.

The sixteen stories in this collection were originally published in the following issues of **Mike Shayne Mystery Magazine:**

Leave it to a Pro (July 1979)
Johnny Ninety (October 1979)
Tickets For the Game (March 1980)
A Blend of Murder (August 1980)
Good Odds For Murder (July 1981)
Water in a Teacup (February 1982)
Mama's Darling (June 1982)
The Habituals (February 1983)
A Matter of Organization (April 1983)
Second Chance (August 1983)
The Fourth Friday (November 1983)
Rocky and the Phantom Lady (February 1984)
Beanball (May 1984)
What Would You Have Done? (July 1984)
A Dog's Best Friend (October 1984)
Father's Girl (aka Missing) (June 1985)

CONTENTS

INTRODUCTION

During its final years Mike Shayne Mystery Magazine had become a repository for stories rejected by the two major publications in the genre, Alfred Hitchcock's and Ellery Queen's mystery magazines. That they had been rejected doesn't mean that many of the stories in Shayne weren't every bit as good as those found in the other two. Some were too rough, too down to earth for the mild Hitchcock and even milder Queen.

Although digest size, in many respects Shayne was the last survivor of the pulp magazines that had thrived during the first half of the 20th century. At that time a dozen or so in the mystery and suspense field alone could be found at any newsstand. There were others to satisfy almost every taste: westerns, romance, adventure, horror, World War I combat in the skies. The majority sold for a dime and the writers made pennies per word.

Some of those early pulp writers are revered today as masters of the craft – Dashiell Hammett, Raymond Chandler, Cornell Woolrich among them. Then there was pulp writer Davis Dresser, who wrote the Michael Shayne stories under the pseudonym Brett Halliday.

The first Shayne book appeared in 1939 after being rejected 22 times. Many others were published before he quit writing them in 1958. After that more appeared under his name but were ghost written. Halliday, who lost an eye as a boy and wore an eye patch, was a prolific pulp writer and used a number of pseudonyms for stories published in various genres. He was a founding member of Mystery Writers of America.

Mike Shayne Mystery Magazine was born in 1956 and survived nearly 30 years until the final issue appeared in August of 1985. My last story was in the June issue that year so it would be unfair to say I killed it off, although I may have helped.

It was a fun publication loaded with tough, cutting edge stories that sometimes included raw language and considerable brutality. Among its writers were the leading names in the field: John Lutz, Edward D. Hoch, Bill Pronzini, Dan J. Marlowe and numerous others. Every issue featured a ghosted Brett Halliday story about the red-headed private eye, Michael Shayne.. In its late years many of them were written by James M. Reasoner and the team of Hal Blythe and Charles Sweet.

My own stories were a mixed bag. Protagonists ranged from private detectives and hardened criminals to a not-so-sweet little girl. Some were pretty good and some, well . . . Sam Merwin, Jr. was the editor when I submitted my first manuscript to Shayne. He sent it back with this note: "Close, but no cigar." A few months later (July 1979) he published *Leave it to a Pro*, the first piece of my fiction to make it into print. Soon after that Charles E. (Chuck) Fritch, who had written for the magazine, became its editor.

For a reason known only to him, Chuck changed the name of *Father's Girl* to *Missing*. That's as insipid as a title can be so I changed it back again for this collection.

Shayne had its downside, of course. Every writer would agree that the pay was so atrociously low that some of those penny-a-word pulp writers of the 1920s and 1930s would have crossed it off their list. I believe the largest check I received was for $125. That's why its stories had always been submitted to better paying markets before finding a home at Mike Shayne. Still many of the tales found in its pages – not necessarily mine – were the equal of any published elsewhere.

So here they are, sixteen of the seventeen stories I had in Mike Shayne Mystery Magazine. I hate the one that's missing, *Footsteps of Death*. Under no conditions would I want it to see the light of day ever again. The others – those found here – were written at a time when I was searching for the ideal protagonist for a series. I found him (or them) in private eye Jack Eddy and his sidekick, police beat newspaper reporter Bram Geary, but by then Mike Shayne had passed into history three years earlier. Had that not been true, Jack and Bram might never have visited Shayne because none of their adventures has been rejected. – DS

LEAVE IT TO A PRO

It began innocently enough. A joke, really. Something to make the dreary hours a little less monotonous. The first evening had been uneventful and now, midway through the second five-hour shift, the assignment had become downright boring.

"Some fun," Bolka grumbled. "Babysitting a bunch of telephones. There's no way those vandals are going to come back with us standing around. If they try to send us back out here tomorrow night I'm really going to raise hell."

He shuffled away, kicked a paper cup lying on the floor, returned to the door where his companion was standing. "Why do you suppose they'd have ten telephone booths in a place like this anyway?" he went on. "1 can't believe there'd ever be that many people calling from here at the same time."

Fredoni shrugged, shaking his head. Bolka was right, he thought. It didn't make sense but the booths were there, nevertheless, and the telephone company was paying the agency to have them watched. They stood In a single row along one wall of a wide, dimly-lit corridor connecting a drug store with a rear parking lot. The lot served several businesses in a small shopping center along the main street linking downtown with the east side Industrial area. Further out it passed through a succession of suburban bedroom communities, each a little more prestigious than the one before.

"You know it's young punks," Bolka droned on. "Even they have enough sense to spot us."

The harsh, bass voice matched George Bolka's big-boned, barrel-shaped body. His appearance alone was enough to send any potential vandals in search of another target. Long arms hung like oversized sausages from wide, flat shoulders and size fourteen shoes didn't look big at all beneath the massive girth of his legs. His face was rectangular, florid, with bushy black brows over squinty black eyes and the squashed nose of a boxer. The unlit stub of a cigar was stuck in one corner of his coarse, thick-lipped mouth. A wide-brimmed black hat and long black overcoat completed an apparition-like picture.

Fredoni was sick of his partner's complaining. Boring jobs were part of working for a large detective agency and the only thing that could be done about it was quit. It wasn't, he often thought, like the life of a television private eye. More often than not the assignments handed out in the morning by an assistant manager turned out to be dull, routine or both. There were exceptions, of course, just often enough to keep him interested.

He stood at the rear door, listlessly watching the few cars that left or entered the parking lot. After several minutes of silence he chuckled and called, "Hey, look at this!" Bolka, quick and agile despite his excess poundage, hurried to the door almost hoping to see a gang of youths approaching, weapons in hand.

"Look at those two," said Fredoni, nodding toward a Cadillac sedan parked to the left of the door. A man and woman, oblivious of their surroundings, were kissing passionately in the front seat.

"Cheaters!" Bolka snorted. "Not too smart about it, either."

"Yeah," agreed Fredoni, still chuckling. "They're asking for trouble.

Anybody could walk out this door and see them." Subconsciously he noted the license number.

The embrace ended and the woman got out. By the time she reached the door, Fredoni was entering the drug store at the far end of the corridor and Bolka was fumbling for change in front of the booths. She walked to a booth halfway along the row. Bolka quietly slipped into one next to her.

She dialed a number, waited a few seconds and said, "Hello, honey. Can you come and get me? I'm at the drug store – Gray's on Euclid." After a short pause she added, "Bring them with you as long as they're still up. I'll be at the back door. Bye now."

Bolka was mumbling into a dead phone as she stepped out of the booth.

She entered the drug store and walked directly to the cosmetic counter, handled an item or two and then checked her makeup in a small, round mirror on the counter. She took a tissue from her purse, wiped her mouth and applied fresh lipstick.

Fredoni, flipping pages of a magazine at a nearby rack, watched her with interest. Good looking, he thought, with the unmistakable air of someone accustomed to money. Bolka walked past him, pausing momentarily to pick up a magazine and whisper, "She called home and her husband and kids are coming to pick her up." Both men grinned.

The woman wandered from counter to counter for a few minutes, paid for several small items at the register and walked the length of the corridor to the rear door. Fredoni moved to the only area of the store where the corridor was visible, pretending to be absorbed in a study of trinkets and impulse sale items.

The headlights of a car illuminated the passageway. The woman opened the door and hurried to it. Fredoni walked to the door and stepped outside in time to see her give the driver a wifely peck on the cheek before turning to two small children in the back seat.

The car, a Lincoln Continental, was backing out when Fredoni reached his battered old Chevrolet. Again he filed the license number in his mind. He walked back inside after the Continental pulled away. Bolka was waiting and the two of them laughed.

"This job," Fredoni said, "all the standing around watching, could give a shakedown artist more work than he could handle."

"Yeah," agreed Bolka, "and don't think it hasn't been done. If you go to the right places and keep your eyes open you can see more than people would ever dream of. Most people are wrapped up in their own thoughts, don't really see what they're looking at. If they did, they wouldn't need us."

Fredoni nodded, took out a small notebook and wrote down the two license numbers. Just for fun he'd check them out the next day.

Fred Fredoni's appearance was a startling contrast to that of his partner. His slender, five-eight frame had a deceptively fragile look. Actually he was rock-hard, muscular. His features were Latin and his slick black hair combed straight back from a sloping forehead was reminiscent of Valentino. There was an aura of poverty about him, though. It showed in his face and in his apparel. His suit was clean and neatly pressed, but off a bargain basement rack. It had been worn too long and so had his shirt, clean but frayed at the collar. His shoes were polished but run over at the heels and, when he crossed his legs, holes were visible in the soles.

His appearance might have been a handicap in a business dependent upon gaining the confidence of strangers. It wasn't, because of a boyish smile that, along with soulful, almost pleading brown eyes, gave him an air of helplessness that brought out the mother instinct in women and affected men in a way that made them want to assist the down-on-his-luck young man if they possibly could.

There hadn't been a day in Fred Fredoni's life when money wasn't a problem. There wasn't enough of it when he was growing up, when he was married for a stormy two years, or particularly after the divorce that left him saddled with weekly support payments for a young daughter. Money was the dominant topic at the dinner table during childhood years in Glenwood, a crowded, tough, east side neighborhood of Poles, Slavs and Italians. His father toiled long hours in the railroad shops and his mother skimped and saved in every way possible but there never seemed to be enough of anything for the Fredonis and their nine children. It was a common affliction of the neighborhood, though, so the youthful Freddie accepted it as a normal part of everyone's life.

14

Only Uncle Angelo had money. He wore expensive clothes, smoked fifty-cent cigars and lived in a semi-luxurious apartment on the avenue. Freddie knew his mother didn't approve of her brother-in-law and from a very early age realized it had to do with Uncle Angelo's business. When he was much older he would learn of organized crime, but in his younger years Freddie knew only that his uncle was part of the Glenwood Gang, something spoken of in hushed voices by children in the neighborhood and never mentioned at all by grown ups.

Sometimes his uncle would slip a dollar bill into Freddie's hand when they were alone. Mussing up the boy's hair, he'd say, "Go buy your self a present from your Uncle Angie, kid, but don't tell your mama." Freddie would keep the secret, feeling guilty. He'd usually take a younger brother or sister with him to the corner confectionery for an unaccustomed treat.

Freddie was nine when Uncle Angelo was gunned down on the sidewalk as he walked to his car in front of the Fredoni house. The barrel of the shotgun being pulled inside the dark blue sedan as it sped away with tires squealing was permanently engraved on the young boy's mind. So was the sight of his uncle's torn body. Freddie, fifty yards away, had been running toward him when the shots were fired. A dollar bill was clutched in his uncle's hand.

Word circulated quickly through the neighborhood. It was the Murray Hill Mob, they whispered on the streets and in the small stores and dreary bars in Glenwood. Years later Freddie would understand that it was the opening fusillade in a territorial war that flourished briefly on the east side and then died as suddenly as it began. At the time he knew only that he hated crime and hated criminals.

His feeling about crime remained unchanged, but his opinion of those involved mellowed in the years after high school as longtime friends drifted into the Glenwood Gang. Boyhood dreams of being fire fighters, baseball players or astronauts died early in the neighborhood. They were replaced by the reality of the auto plant assembly lines, the steel mills down in the flats or, for some, the Glenwood Gang.

The morning after the stakeout, his huge body quivering with indignation, Bolka protested as promised when told he and Fredoni would be back at the same stand that evening.

"It'll be your last night," a young, tense assistant manager assured them, "regardless of how long the assignment goes."

Bolka grunted in annoyance when each of them was handed another unpopular task, checking out an applicant for the agency's guard department.

It was a two- or three-hour job and the result was a foregone conclusion; if the applicant was breathing and didn't have a police record, he qualified. The pay was too low to set the standards higher.

"That leaves the whole afternoon to kill," Bolka complained, leaning forward in his chair and drumming the fat fingers of one hand on the assistant manager's desk. "How about a theater check?"

The assistant manager, always intimidated by Bolka, shuffled the papers on his desk, mumbled, "We don't have one scheduled until tomorrow."

Bolka extended his hand. "Give it to me," he said. "I'll do it today and date it tomorrow."

"You know we're not supposed to do that, the assistant manager whined, but he made no effort to retrieve the assignment sheet Bolka had snatched from his hand. Bolka grunted again, folded the paper and put it in his jacket pocket. It amounted to little more than getting paid for watching a free movie.

Fredoni laughed inwardly at Bolka's heavy-handed domination of the assistant manager. He was content himself with having the afternoon free. The license numbers in his notebook were on his mind although he would have been at a loss to explain why. Something about the casual way the man and woman seemed to flaunt their affair irritated him. Their meetings should have been furtive, clandestine, but to Fredoni it appeared that their big, expensive cars, their money, made them feel superior to that sort of thing. They were arrogant about it and he detested arrogance.

A clerk at the main police station, a shapely, auburn-haired woman of thirty or so, supplied the information he wanted. She

16

handed him two file cards on which she had written names and addresses, snickered and said, "Don't tell me my doctor's in trouble."

Fredoni glanced at the name on the top card: Phillip Carey, M.D.

"Just checking an insurance claim," he said. "You know him?"

"Not really, but I went to his office a few times a year ago. He has the biggest weight-control program in the city and I wanted to lose a few pounds."

Fredoni's gaze began at her ankles and moved upward. From where, he wondered. "Then you do know him, " he said.

"Well, I saw him for a minute or two each time, if that's what you mean, but I don't really know him. It's the kind of place where you give your name to the receptionist, wait your turn and then just tell the doctor you want to lose weight. A nurse gives you a packet of pills on your way out."

"No examination or anything?"

"He weighs you," she said, "but that's about it."

Fredoni thanked her and walked out, seething inside. Legalized dope peddling, he thought. Kids on the street get sent up for it but if you have a diploma on the wall it's okay.

In the lobby he lit a cigarette and looked at the second card. Ralph L. Brown, the owner of the Continental, lived in an exclusive suburb a few miles from the drug store. He walked into another office, opened a city directory on the counter and turned to the B's. He studied one listing a moment, flipped the book shut and walked out. Brown was plant manager of an auto manufacturer's local stamping plant. His wife's name was Margaret. The library of the city's morning newspaper was Fredoni's next stop.

The librarian, a thin spinster without makeup, hair in a tight bun and wearing large, round glasses was, like the clerk at the police station, a cultivated acquaintance. Her files often were very useful to him. After a minute or two of preliminary conversation she asked, "What can I help you with today, Mr. Fredoni?"

"Ralph L. Brown and his wife, Margaret," he said. "Know them?"

"That would be Maggie Brown, I believe. Very active socially and in charitable work. Let me get the file."

"See if you have one on Dr. Phillip Carey while you' re back there."

She did, a thin one. A few honors, mention of the usual medical organizations, a story announcing Carey's plans to build an office complex several years earlier. He was married and had two children.

Brown's envelope was jammed with clippings, thanks to Maggie. She apparently was involved in any project likely to get her name in the paper. There were a few business-related clippings on Brown, but his major role, if newspaper lineage meant anything, was escorting Maggie to an endless round of charity balls, theater openings and celebrity get-togethers.

Fredoni repeated the insurance claim story to the librarian, thanked her, gave her the hoped-for up-and-down appraisal while she smiled self- consciously and patted the back of her hair, and then left.

Outside again, he stood contemplating his next move, ignoring a cold, misty rain and savoring the fresh air. He had found out all he wanted to know. There was no reason to return to the office, it was too early to go back to the drug store but too late to bother driving to his dingy, furnished apartment. He fingered the loose change in his pocket, decided he could afford one beer if he ate only a sandwich for supper, and dodged traffic to get to a bar across the street.

He nursed the beer, making it last as long as possible because he had nothing to do and nowhere to go. His thoughts were bitter, right in tune with the dark, lowering sky outside. A couple of winners, he said to himself. A quack who pockets a fortune peddling pills to unhappy housewives so they can get high on the amphetamines, and a broad who blows her husband's money as fast as he can make it and still isn't satisfied.

His increasingly black moods were beginning to bother him. He had to do something to snap out of it, he knew, but he had no idea what it would be. Bust your butt, he thought, and still barely make it from paycheck to paycheck. His agency salary was pathetically low and they even took advantage of the investigators on expenses, expecting them to drive their cars but paying only bus fare to and from downtown.

He had considered going on secret, what they called an undercover assignment on TV or in detective stories. It meant working in a factory, a warehouse, a packing plant, but on secret you kept your full paycheck from the job plus receiving half of your agency salary. He hated secrets, though. It was always some menial, boring, back-breaking job and usually meant playing stool pigeon. Still he had to do something. Like having the state issue him a license to steal, he thought angrily. But Glenwood High hadn't handed out the right kind of diploma.

"Hi, kid," Bolka said as he walked into the drug store at the precise moment a nearby church bell began tolling six o'clock. "God, I don't know if I can take another night of this or not."

"At least it's the last one," muttered Fredoni. How, he wondered, did his partner support a wife and two children, drive a late model car and maintain a house in a pretty decent neighborhood on his agency pay? Maybe he really did do a little shaking down. On the other hand, Bolka didn't impress him as sharp enough to pull it off.

Still treating it lightly, Fredoni told Bolka about the doctor and his lover. He decided to test the big man. "It would be a snap to muscle them for a little," he said. "They wouldn't miss it, that's for sure."

"That's risky stuff you're talking about, kid," Bolka said, shaking his head. "You could get killed that way."

"You could this way, too," Fredoni replied curtly, jerking his head in the direction of the phone booths.

Bolka looked at them. "Yeah," he said, "you've got a point there."

The hours dragged by again, even more slowly than the first two nights. The rain had gotten heavier and then became mixed with snow so even the customers stayed away. It allowed too much time for thinking. Fredoni, as the interminable minutes ticked away, grew increasingly distraught. His problems seemed like a vise, squeezing him until he wanted to cry out against the injustices life handed out.

Bolka, who had spent most of the evening in the pharmacist's enclosure reading confession magazines off the rack, shuffled along the corridor as the end of the shift neared. Fredoni turned as he approached. He laughed, but there was little mirth in it.

"Not even a Dr. Carey to liven it up tonight," he said. Then, without realizing he was going to, he added, "Damn, I'd like to shake that SOB down a little."

"Too risky, Freddie," Bolka said. "You'd be out on the street if the agency found out. You might even wind up behind bars or, like 1 said, get yourself killed."

"1 know it," Fredoni snarled. "I'm just talking, you know that."

Bolka gave him a long, penetrating look. "Sure, kid," he said softly. "Sure."

A week passed before they met again while waiting for assignments one morning in the office. It had been seven days of mental turmoil for Fredoni.

"Had anything interesting lately?" Bolka asked.

"Nothing," Fredoni replied. "God, it's been slow. They even had me out practicing surveillances one afternoon. I practiced on a guy sitting at a bar."

Bolka chuckled. "Good thinking, kid," he said. "It's been quiet for me, too. Don't let it get to you."

Crap, thought Fredoni. Seeing Bolka again had added to his tension. He walked to the lone window in the investigators' room, studied the traffic seven floors below for a few minutes and then slumped down in a chair at the opposite end of the room from Bolka. He studied the big man out of the corners of his eyes. Bolka had taken off his overcoat. His suit was well-tailored, his shirt collar crisp, his black shoes expensive.

How the hell does he do it, Fredoni asked himself. He has to be knocking down on the side. I wonder – has the big slob gone ahead and put the touch on the doctor after all his talk about it being too risky? If he has, it means it isn't his first shakedown.

It was on his mind the rest of the day. Finally, alone in his apartment late in the evening, he reached a decision. He would call Carey himself. If Bolka had been there before him the doctor was certain to give it away.

Fredoni didn't realize it, but it was the excuse he had subconsciously been seeking. He wouldn't be shaking anyone down – the word blackmail was too dirty, it was blocked from his mind – he would be checking to see if a fellow investigator was nothing but a crook masquerading as a detective.

Convincing the receptionist that she should put his call through to the doctor was no problem for someone accustomed to the daily use of pretexts. This time, however, his palms and upper lip were sweating. There was a short delay, a click, a brusque voice saying, "Doctor Carey."

Fredoni cleared his throat, hesitated, finally said hoarsely, "1 have something important to discuss with you, doctor. Because of its nature I think we should talk alone after your office hours."

"Out of the question," snapped Carey. "I never do it. Either tell me your business now or make an appointment with my receptionist."

"It would be to your advantage to do it my way, Doc," Fredoni said. He felt sure of himself again. Carey's high-handed attitude infuriated him. Slowly, so the words would sink in, he said, "I'm sure Maggie Brown would agree with me."

There was a lengthy pause before Carey said, "What did you say?"

"You heard me, Doc."

Another pause and then, "All right, come at seven o'clock. Knock on the outer door."

"Fine, Doctor. See you at seven." Fredoni replaced the receiver, smiling.

It was so simple. One-thousand dollars. Back in his shabby apartment he counted it again, spreading the bills out on a wobbly kitchen table. They were small denominations, soiled, untraceable. He had pulled the figure out of the air and the doctor, without argument, had taken the money from a safe concealed in a closet off his main treatment room.

Carey had turned out to be exactly what Fredoni expected. He had studied him closely, first as they talked briefly in the doctor's inner office   and then as Carey crouched over the small safe. The doctor impressed Fredoni as the composite of all the things he had grown to detest in recent months. He was handsome, but in a characterless, insubstantial way that marked him as a person who never had been forced to cope with real adversity. He was a product of indulgent parents, wealthy suburbs, exclusive schools and luxurious country clubs. Life as it was lived in Glenwood would be totally alien to him, completely beyond his comprehension and therefore, in his mind, inferior.

The doctor, to Fredoni, was like many of the agency's clients; self-centered, greedy, dishonest, but dishonest in a socially acceptable way. He didn't burglarize houses, he didn't enter stores with a gun in his hand and a mask on his face, he didn't belong to organized crime's hierarchy, but still, in Fredoni's mind, he was as crooked as any of those who did. The only difference was that Carey, through no doing of his own, had been born into a way of life that made the other things unnecessary.

Fredoni saw greed, selfishness, a man weak because of the very things he believed made him strong.   What Fredoni overlooked was the latent threat of a man accustomed to having his own way when he felt his secure world endangered.

Carey had asked no questions, not even the name of his visitor, so Fredoni – Tony Wells if a name were needed – had one of his own. "Anything like this ever happen before, Doc?" he asked.

"Certainly not."   Carey paused in counting the money, fixed Fredoni with a cold stare. And it better not again."

"Don't worry, Doc, it's a one-shot deal."

"I really hope you mean that." Carey emphasized each word.

Fredoni made certain he wasn't followed when he left the office and walked to his car parked in a shopping center several blocks away. God, he thought, it was so easy. Guilt deep within him was buried by a sense of elation, of power. It was justice, really. The doctor deserved it.

Maggie Brown saw no justice in the way Carey abruptly ended their affair. She was furious, more so because he didn't even offer an explanation. Her reaction convinced Carey she had not been contacted by the blackmailer. He made his plans accordingly.

Fredoni meant it when he told Carey he would not return for more. Had he been honest with himself he would have known better. He was familier with the base motives that make work for private detectives and he was well aware that greed ranks as a prime mover. He had never crossed the line before, but once the first step is taken it is easier to go ahead than turn back.

The money merely whet his appetite for more. It went fast; a couple of suits, a few shirts, a pair of shoes, some work on his car, dinners at decent restaurants for a change. It had seemed like so much and suddenly it was gone.

He thought of approaching Maggie Brown but rejected the idea. Women were too emotional, unpredictable. When he called Carey the second time, guilt smoldered inside Fredoni. He could no longer pretend that he was checking on a fellow investigator, but he still fooled himself by thinking of it as a shakedown. The real word for it remained blocked from his mind.

The same arrangements were made for the second meeting. As soon as Carey was alone in his office he began preparations according to plan. He took a heavy wrench from the supply room toolbox and put it in his jacket pocket. An injection was prepared in the treatment room and a thirty-eight revolver was transferred from a locked cabinet in his private office to the center drawer of his desk. Finished, he leaned back in his chair, lit a cigarette, and waited.

"Hi, Doc," Fredoni said when Carey let him in. Without speaking, the doctor locked the door again and led the way directly to the treatment room. Cabinets lined one wall of the large room that contained an examination table, several wheeled tables loaded with paraphernalia, a cot and three chairs.

"Sit down," Carey said, indicating a chair near the center of the room with a toss of his head. He walked behind it to the door of the closet where the safe was hidden.

Fredoni was uncomfortable, embarrassed by what he was doing. It was a voluntary act but it wasn't something he relished. Only the result – the money – was enjoyable.

He started to turn in his chair, said, "Look, Doc –" He halted in mid-sentence, drew back hastily. Not in time, though, to avoid the wrench. Carey's blow was aimed at his right temple, but Fredoni's sudden move caused the wrench to glance off his shoulder. He jumped to his feet in a crouched position, swinging at the same time.

The off-balance punch caught the side of Carey's jaw. He stumbled backward, caught himself, lunged again toward the smaller man. Fredoni warded off the second swing of the wrench with his left forearm and aimed another punch at the doctor's midsection. It hit with little force at the same instant Carey's wrench connected with the left side of the detective's forehead. The blow wasn't solid but it was enough to drop Fredoni to his knees. Carey let go of the wrench and delivered a knockout punch with his fist.

The doctor stood still a moment, inhaling deeply. His script hadn't been followed but the result was as good, he decided. Better, perhaps. With Fredoni out, he returned to his original plan. The injection was administered and then, grasping Fredoni under both arms, Carey dragged him to the nearest wall and propped him against it in a sitting position. The doctor, kneeling in front of Fredoni, struck him several more times with his fist, loosened his necktie and ripped open the top button of his new Van Heusen shirt. Carey then went to work on himself. Fredoni's blows made it easier.

It had scraped the skin on the side of his jaw so redness and a slight swelling were visible. When satisfied with his own appearance, Carey began upsetting and breaking things until it appeared that a wild melee had taken place in the room. He then went into his adjoining private office and did the same.

The next step was the hardest. Carey selected a sharp knife from a tray of instruments and, without allowing himself time to think about it, thrust it into his left arm below and to the outside of the elbow. He cried out involuntarily, withdrew the blade and placed the knife back on the table with only the handle touching the surface.

The doctor then lifted Fredoni to his feet and half dragging, half carrying the unconscious man, took him into the private office. With considerable difficulty Carey braced the detective against one end of the desk, supporting him with his left hand. With his right hand he opened the desk drawer and picked up the gun. Still holding Fredoni's right arm with his left hand, Carey carefully gauged the angle. His hand was shaking when he squeezed the trigger but his aim was true. Fredoni jerked violently and that, along with the unexpected loudness of the shot in the small room, caused Carey to release his grip. A red stain was spreading across the left side of his tan shirt when Fredoni's lifeless body hit the floor.

Carey paused only a moment to look at the result of his work. He walked quickly into the treatment room, picked up the knife, wiped several spots of blood from the floor with his handkerchief, returned to his office, cleaned the knife handle and carefully placed it in his victim's right hand. He ticked things off in his mind, made a hasty survey of the two rooms and then, satisfied he had overlooked nothing, called the police.

"We had a real fight when I wouldn't give him what he wanted," Carey said to conclude his story to a slender, small-featured homicide detective. "If I hadn't been able to get to the gun I don't know how it would have ended. He was sky high, strong as an ox for a man his size. It's reaching the point where a doctor doesn't dare keep drugs in his office."

"Ummm," murmured Lieutenant Rubin Steinmetz. He stroked his pencil-thin mustache with one finger and to himself thought, "Bull!" The story was phony. He didn't say so but Carey could read it in his face.

The autopsy revealed the presence of the drug and the entry and exit wounds were consistent with the doctor's story. Carey's own wound was one that might have been suffered by a man attempting to ward off a knife thrust, but still Steinmetz knew it all was contrived, a hoax. He also knew he couldn't prove it.

Carey was smiling to himself as he walked away from a brief coroner's inquest several days later. Justifiable was the ruling, as he knew it would be. Self defense. Even Steinmetz's steady, penetrating stare, obviously intended to let

Carey know the case wasn't closed in his mind, didn't disturb the doctor.

He arrived at his office, closed since the shooting, shortly after workmen finished cleaning up and replacing the bloodstained carpet. Carey unwrapped a cigar, sat down and leaned back in his big desk chair, lit the cigar and exhaled a cloud of smoke.

"Perfect," he said aloud. "Just perfect." He was content, relaxed, self- satisfied. He propped his feet on the desk, stared at the ceiling and to himself thought: Steinmetz didn't buy the story but it's all instinct on his part. There's not a damn thing he can do about it. So much for Mister Blackmailer – it's over and done with.

The ringing of the telephone jarred Carey from his reverie. He debated whether to answer it, decided there was no reason not to.

"Good job, Doctor," said the deep voice on the other end of the line. "You didn't fool Steinmetz, you know, but he's helpless unless something new breaks for him."

Carey dropped his feet to the floor, straightened up in the chair, let the cigar fall into an ashtray. "Who is this?" he said huskily.

"Just a mutual friend. Of yours and Freddie's that is. Oh, and Maggie, of course." The words were followed by a humorless chuckle.

Stunned, Carey gripped the edge of the desk with his free hand. The room was spinning around before his eyes. Finally, after a long delay, he said, "What do you want?"

I think we need to reach some sort of agreement, don't you, Doctor?"

"What do you mean, agreement?"

"Nothing of consequence to a man of your position. Say five hundred a month. Cash. In small, used, unmarked bills. Mailed the first of every month to John Jones, Box 1347, at the main post office."

"I don't know . . ." Carey's voice trailed away. He couldn't believe it was happening.

"Yes you do, Doctor. Remember Steinmetz. If he had the link connecting you with . . ."

"Okay, okay," interrupted Carey. "We'll do as you say."

"I knew you were a reasonable man, Doctor. Now there's one more thing. Just in case you'd think of trying to track me down through the post office box or some other way, there's something you should know. Half an hour ago I deposited with my attorney a sealed envelope to be opened in the event of my death. An inner envelope is addressed to Steinmetz and I think you know what it contains. Keep In mind there is no statute of limitation on murder."

"Just a minute," Carey stammered. "What if you get hit by a truck or have a heart attack?"

"I guess that's something you'll just have to hope doesn't happen. Chalk it up to the risks of the business. Should make reading the obituaries an interesting guessing game for you, right?"

Bolka laughed aloud as he hung up the phone. Amateurs. Fredoni and Carey, a couple of amateurs. The big blackmailer and the man who committed the perfect murder. A couple of punks, that's all. They should have left such things to a real pro.

He was still laughing when he stepped from the booth into the corridor as a youth ripped the receiver from a phone several booths away.

"Hey, Punk!" Bolka shouted. "I mean you, kid!"

He lunged at the vandal, collaring him just as a second youth stepped from a booth behind Bolka and delivered a crushing blow to his head with a section of iron pipe.

The crowd gathered quickly. A man wearing a pharmacist's jacket bent over, looked at Bolka's face and said, "That's one of the private detectives that was here a few weeks ago watching the phones. He must have come back on his own and caught somebody in the act."

"If he did, it was a mistake," said the man kneeling beside the body. "He's dead, better call the police."

This drawing that fit the mood of the story accompanied *Johnny Ninety* in Mike Shayne Mystery Magazine.

JOHNNY NINETY

It wasn't much of a ski slope, not to someone accustomed to spending winter weekends at Whiteface Mountain or Killington. It was outdoors, though, and that's what mattered, that's all he really wanted.   That and a chance to be alone, feel the wind in his face, give it a chance to clear the smoke, the stale air, the jaded thoughts from his mind.

One run down the easy main slope was enough for Clary, but he wasn't ready to go inside.   A bar stool in the lodge held no appeal, not yet anyway, and the special bus wouldn't make its next trip back to Cleveland for another hour, so he jumped aboard the chair lift and rode to the top again.

Beginner and intermediate slopes, hazy under bright floodlights, were off to his left.   He wanted no part of them or the noisy, laughing people using them.   People – he'd had more than enough of people for one day.   For many days, in fact.

Business, too.   He'd had enough of that for a while.   Long meetings in musty hotel conference rooms.   The never-ending problems to be tackled, thrashed out and solved when he was home in Albany.   The irritation with David Boylen, the wondering when he'd begin holding up his end of the partnership.

For what?   The question arose in his mind almost daily now. For more money?   Maybe.   It once had been the most important thing in the world to him.   At the beginning it was the thought of the things it could buy, the things it would enable him to do. Then somewhere along the way it became just the earning of it, the raking it in, that satisfied him. Now he wasn't sure what it was, not since that day three months ago. His birthday. His thirtieth.

It was just another day, of course. He'd stopped looking forward to birthdays years ago. Something about this one was different, though. He was uneasy from the time he got up in the morning, couldn't concentrate on business, wasn't anticipating the evening with pleasure, not even the small party Dorene had planned. It was a clear, crisp October day, the kind that always made him wish it was Saturday and a good football game was around.

He had gotten up suddenly, right in the middle of a conference, left the office and walked the streets nearly three hours. Was this it? At the age of thirty was he locked into a routine for life? Why? For more money to buy things he didn't really care about? More money to feed a marriage that long-since had become boring to both parties? More money just so he could make more money and more and more and more?

He went back. He always did. For a while he had toyed with the idea of not doing so but he went back, back without the answers. But since then the questions kept intruding on his thoughts more and more often.

The hell with all that, he thought, easing off the chair lift and gliding across the hard-packed snow. No reason to go right back down again, he'd explore a little. Not that there was all that much territory to explore. The top of the hill was level and cleared of trees for a good hundred yards to the north. To the west and south were the slopes – something to avoid – and to the east the dark outline of a woods.

He headed north and quickly covered the length of the clearing. Looking down he could see the headlights of cars on an interstate highway, and in the distance the gray expense he knew was Lake Erie. He stood there a few moments, watching the lights and listening to the wind moaning in the treetops to his right. Then he began moving again, this time toward the trees.

He skirted the edge of the woods, tempted to push on in and lose himself in its loneliness, leave so-called civilization behind for a while. He didn't, he never gave in to such impulses. Maybe that was the trouble.

He continued south until the trees became sparse as he neared the lights of the main slope. There he found a gentle descent, the same as that of the main slope but a route that wove downward among the scattered oaks, maples and firs. Again he was tempted. Why not glide down the incline alone through the trees rather than on the garish, crowded slope? It was light enough, no problem there. Easy, too, for anyone other than a rank beginner. He shouldn't, but for once he was going to yield to an impulse, be unconventional. He pushed off.

It was a smooth trip down, weaving in and out among the widely-spaced trees with just enough speed to make it exciting, satisfying. A phantom bobbing back and forth, silently moving along without disturbing nature's solitude.

The ravine was twenty feet deep and twenty-five feet across. The gentle rises and depressions hid it from him, concealed it until he was right on top of it. There was nothing he could do, nothing but glide off the edge and sail almost majestically through the air. He wasn't going fast enough to clear it, not even close. He was aware of dropping at the same time momentum carried him forward and then was conscious of a brilliant burst of gold and silver. Then nothing.

He was disoriented, confused. Heavy fog, more like dense clouds, surrounded him, cut him off from everything. He was lying on his back, aware of pain in his right arm and shoulder. His head hurt, too, so he raised his left hand to try to brush the swirling white mist from his eyes. For a moment it receded but then closed in again. He repeated the move several times and each time the mist seemed to clear a little until, with a start, he realized two white-robed, ghostly figures were hovering beyond his feet.

He closed his eyes, thought about it. Small evergreens, probably, covered with snow. When he was fully awake he'd be able to see them clearly. He kept his eyes closed, deliberately counted to one hundred, and opened them again. The mist was still there and so were the apparitions. As he watched, one slowly drifted away but returned in a moment with a third, taller figure also draped in white. He shut his eyes again as the tallest of the menacing forms left the other two and moved closer.

When he opened them once more the fog was almost gone. Clary sighed, aware now that he was lying in a bed and the frightening figures were nothing more than a doctor and two nurses. The doctor, bending over him and smiling, said, "Feeling better?"

Clary nodded a little. Better than what?

The doctor, straightening up, said, "Rest a while longer and then I'll be back." Clary started to protest but the mist began closing in again so he didn't care.

Bright sunshine flooded the room when he awoke. The pain was still there but the mist was gone and his head felt better. He remembered the run down the uncharted slope and swore softly to himself. What a stupid thing to do. The sun was high, it must be close to noon, and his conference was to have resumed at nine. He needed a telephone, saw one but it was out of reach and when he tried to move, the pain intensified. He found a call button and pushed it.

A nurse opened the door, smiled and said, "Be right with you." She shut the door again but returned in a few minutes with the doctor and an older woman dressed in street clothes.

"Well, you look much better," the doctor said. "It's nothing too serious so don't be concerned. Your arm and collarbone are broken and you suffered a concussion but you'll be back on your feet in no time."

"I have to use the phone," Clary said, "and has my wife been notified?"

The older woman moved closer, said, "We have a problem there. You had no identification when you were admitted."

"Damn!" Clary said. "That's right, I left everything in a locker at the ski lodge."

The woman's eyebrows lifted and the doctor looked puzzled. "Ski lodge?" he said. "In Galveston?"

"Galveston?" Clary echoed. What was the man talking about? He'd never been in Galveston in his life. Never been

32

in Texas. If he was joking it was a poor time and place. "What day is this?" he asked.

"Friday," the doctor and the woman said in unison.

"Friday?" Clary repeated, shaking his head. "It was Monday night. You mean I've been out three days?"

The doctor and woman looked at each other. She turned back to Clary and said, "No, you were brought in last evening about eight. I don't know what this is about a ski lodge, you were hit by a car, but there are a few matters we have to straighten out. We need your name and address and have to know how the bill will be paid."

Clary's transition from confusion to anger was swift. "My name's Mitchell Clary," he snarled. "I live in Albany and don't worry about your damn money, you'll be paid. Now I want that telephone moved over here and I want some privacy!"

His bravado faded when he was alone. A lead ball was forming in the pit of his stomach. Where was he, really? What was going on? He was too tired, too confused to cope with it. He stared blankly at the wall a few minutes, the lead ball continuing to grow. Was he still out, caught up in some sort of crazy dream? He reached for the phone, hesitated, afraid to proceed, but finally began pressing buttons.

"Dorene?" he said when the woman answered. There was no response so he repeated, "Dorene?"

"Who is this?" The voice was wary, suspicious.

"It's me, Mitch."

She gasped and her voice quivered when she said, "Mitch? Is this supposed to be a joke? If it is, it isn't funny."

"For God's sake, Dorene what's the matter? I haven't called for a few days but there's been a good reason."

Her laugh was almost hysterical. "It really is you, Mitch, isn't it? You drop off the end of the earth for fifteen months and then say it's been a few days. That's pretty far out, Mitch, even for you."

"Damn it, Dorene," he said, irritated again, "I'm in no mood for games. I've had an accident and guess I'm still groggy. What's happened about the meeting? Have you heard anything?"

"What meeting?"

"The Cleveland meeting! Did David fly down and take over for me? Who's handling the business?"

There was a long pause and her voice was shaky again when she said, "Mitch, there is no business. I don't understand this at all. David sold the business, or what was left of it, six months ago."

He let the phone fall to his side. It was crackling, still, but he didn't hear it. After a few moments he dropped the receiver on the hook. My God, he thought, what's happening? This was no dream. No, it was a nightmare. A weird, incomprehensible nightmare.

The wind off the lake slammed the door behind him, shoving him toward the lobby. He wasn't ready to go there so he braced his legs, turned left into the taproom. Cleveland, he decided as he climbed onto a stool, wasn't his favorite city. Apparently the city wasn't too fond of him, either. Oh well, his calls were completed and he'd be leaving in the morning.

He took a healthy swig from the glass the bartender had placed before him, filled a knobby Savinelli from a roll-up pouch, struck a match and held the flame over the bowl, drawing it in with short, jerky puffs. He sat back, savoring the flavor of the tobacco, the warmth of the room, the first glow of the drink.

Mitch Clary was content. He had wondered about it, his first trip back to Cleveland since the accident. It hadn't bothered him, not at all. As for the rest of it, he certainly felt no sorrow because of the drastic changes in his life in the two years since his last visit. The nine months, really. At least that's what it was in his mind.

That was the only sour note, the one thing that bothered him. Not the loss of the business, certainly. Good riddance, he had become a slave to it. He was happier as a manufacturer's representative. Let someone else have the headaches. And not the divorce, either. He didn't regret that any more than Dorene did. So he walked away from it with little more than the clothes on his back, so what? Starting over again, beginning with new, more modest goals, had been exciting, a thrill he still felt after six months. Money didn't matter, just so he

34

had enough to get by on.

No, it was none of that. The thing that bothered him was the fifteen-month gap in his life, the period erased from his mind like writing vanishes when a wet cloth is run across a chalk board. It still seemed unreal, something that wouldn't happen in real life. Not his life, anyway. He had tried for a while, followed the advice of the doctors, took drugs, underwent hypnosis, all the rest of it. It hadn't helped, so he walked away from it, quit trying. Maybe it would come back in its own time. Maybe it wouldn't.

The lack of identification puzzled him at first. He could understand it when he was on the ski slope, but why would he be walking the streets of a strange city more than a year later without any? The other man, the one who had taken over his mind and body for awhile, had been well groomed, attired in expensive clothing, not some drifter who stepped into the path of a car and was left lying when it sped away.

The police report provided the answer. Two witnesses saw the first man to reach him pinch his wallet and sprint away. If that hadn't happened there'd be no mystery. Something in the wallet would have fanned a spark that would have brought it all back.

He thought it would, anyway. He signaled for another drink, relit his pipe and mulled it over for the thousandth time. Did he really want it to come back now? He wasn't sure. Maybe there was something about that other man he'd rather not know. It frightened him sometimes, knowing a total stranger shared his body. He had thought something in Cleveland might strike the right chord and make it all come rushing back. It hadn't, and now he'd leave in the morning. A day in Akron and another in Pittsburgh and he'd return home. He'd never been in either city so maybe when he left Cleveland behind he might, at last, leave the stranger behind, too.

Clary tossed his suitcase in the trunk, pulled out of the hotel garage, drove a few blocks to the Interstate-77 ramp and headed south. The sun was a hazy yellow ball, a loser in its battle to cut through the murk blanketing the steel mills, the desolate neighborhoods of decrepit buildings and ramshackle houses he passed through. It finally won out when he left the city behind and drove through low, rolling hills to the Ohio Turnpike, took it east to the next exit and continued toward Akron on Route 8.

It had clouded over by the time he saw the needle-like tower looking like some giant lighthouse in the sky. The Cathedral of Tomorrow, he thought, so he was almost there. He had traveled another hundred yards when it hit him, chilled him like a dash of ice water in the face. How had he known it was the tower at the cathedral? It wasn't in Akron, really, it was in Cuyahoga Falls, and he knew that, too. But how? He had never been there.

For an instant he believed he had it. Telecasts from the cathedral went everywhere. He must have seen one, seen the tower, stored it away somewhere. But no, that couldn't be it. He had never watched Rex Humbard's program, he was sure of that.

There were more of them, anyway. It was a frightening feeling, somehow knowing that just ahead he'd make a sweeping curve to the right, swing back left down into a small valley and then up again to find the cathedral on his right and a shopping complex on the left. He drove it exactly as he knew he would, the lead ball he'd had in his stomach nine months ago coming back again, growing steadily larger.

He wheeled into the lot of a small, box-like restaurant a few blocks south of the cathedral, went inside, ordered coffee and lit a cigarette. He inhaled deeply, let the smoke trickle out through his nose, took a drink of the strong, dark brew.

"You've come home," he said to himself, to the hazy shadow sharing his body. But who are you? I still don't know. He chuckled aloud and the counterman turned, stared at him. Now, he realized, Mitch Clary was the stranger. The other man was on familiar ground, not him. He didn't know where he was but the other man did. He would take over now. Maybe a man would walk through the door and say hello or a woman would rush up and throw her arms around him. Not around Mitch Clary, around the other man. But who was he? A shiver traveled along Clary's spine and his palms and upper lip were clammy. He was afraid. More so than he could ever remember being.

His business, his one call, was completed in an hour. Drive right on to Pittsburgh, he told himself, spend the night there,

36

get away from this place. Everything was familiar in an eerie, uncomfortable way. Kind of like watching a travelogue over and over until the streets, the buildings were as recognizable as those at home. He knew the city and yet it was totally impersonal. Like suddenly dropping into some weird science-fiction story, like walking through a dream world.

No, he couldn't leave like that. It would haunt him always, dominate his thoughts, eventually lure him back again. He had to at least try to unravel the tangled mess in his mind. It wasn't noon yet so he would devote the rest of the day and evening to it. Then, if nothing happened, he would be able to live with it, know he had done everything he could.

He wasn't hungry – the lead weight had taken over his stomach – but he forced himself to eat a sandwich and then aimlessly drove the streets. He didn't know what he was looking for, not really. A building, maybe, or a house or a store. Anything that would remove it from the abstract, give it life, body, meaning.

Again he was frustrated. After several hours he stopped for coffee, sat quietly and tried to let his mind drift where it wanted, uncontrolled. Maybe it would slip into some channel he couldn't find through conscious effort. It worked, to a point. Aside from a few main streets most of the neighborhoods were strange, unfamiliar, but something about the east side of the city was pulling on him, drawing his thoughts back as though by magnetism. The big clock in the tower at the Goodyear plant, the bank facing him at an angle where the boulevard took off to the northeast, the shabby business blocks, the expressway above street level in front of the General Tire factory, the road that lead south to the airport. Even the Rubber Bowl, Derby Downs and the huge dirigible hanger, a haunting reminder of an era long past.

Clary checked into a motel just east of downtown near the university. He freshened up, had a drink in the lounge, and then drove again to East Akron. Another hour of cruising accomplished nothing so he stopped at a restaurant on Market Street and ate dinner.

A cold, misty rain was falling when he stepped outside. He drove a few blocks west, parked again and began walking, his coat collar turned up against the rain, but his head unprotected. The moisture created a spectral halo around each street light, every neon sign, added to the loneliness, the apprehension inside him. So did the singing from the street as the tires of passing cars squeezed the wetness from the pavement. The few pedestrians hurrying along, heads down, passed him without acknowledging his existence

Nothing was open but the taverns, dreary workingmen's bars like those in any industrial area. Unhappy places, one not much different than another, as though the clientele brought the monotony of their jobs along with them. Clary entered one at random, found a dozen men seated at a long bar in the gloom. No one looked up when the opening door broke the silence. No one cared if he came in, cared if he stayed or not, so after a few seconds he turned and left.

He was discouraged, ready to give up. He had tried, hadn't he? What more was there to do? He crossed the street, headed back toward his car, walked east past the old plant and newer offices of Goodyear. After several blocks he could see his car and across from it, on his side of the street, another tavern, a cafe, larger than those nearer the factory behind him. It was on a corner, its double wooden doors angled so the entry faced both streets. A pair of globed lights flanked the doors, two yellow eyes drawing him to them.

A faded red arrow was painted above the doors and that, he knew, was the name of the place: The Red Arrow. He knew, too, what he'd find beyond the doors. A cigarette machine and jukebox along the right wall and then a bar that curved and ran the length of the wall facing the door, ending when it came to other doors leading to the kitchen and rest rooms. Booths lining both walls to the left, a small dance floor and tables with checkered clothes in the open area.

They couldn't tell, those already inside, that his heart was pounding, his breathing all out of kilter because someone had shoved the lead ball up from his stomach to the spot where his throat met his chest. He tried to cover it up, appear at ease, nonchalant. He didn't look at anyone, not so their eyes met anyway, so he was unaware that three pairs of them zeroed in on his face and never wavered.

It was exactly as he pictured it, exactly as he knew it would be. Couples, with eyes only for each other, were at a few tables and in a few booths. Several men were clustered around a woman seated at the bar to his right and half a dozen more were scattered along the bar beyond the curve. The four stools at the left were empty so he walked to them and slid onto the one second from the end. A girl was standing alone where the bar ended and the doorways began. He didn't look at her.

A drink was set before him. He didn't remember ordering it and started to say so when the bartender said, "Compliments of Arnie," and jerked his head to Clary's right.

He turned and looked. A tall, muscular, olive-skinned man stared back at him from cold eyes above a twisted grin. He nodded almost imperceptibly and Clary returned it, raised the glass and took a drink. When he looked again the man was reaching over the bar for a telephone.

It was so damned aggravating, so inexplicable. How could he know the place but not the faces? Why should inanimate objects have meaning, be familiar, but not the people? He lit a cigarette and, as he returned the lighter to his pocket, turned to his left. The girl was staring at him, stunned, shocked, as though he were some sort of apparition, the Ghost of Evenings Past.

She was pretty. Not Hollywood beautiful, not artificial like something cast from a mold that turns out endless duplicates. Just pretty. Fresh, wholesome, different than girls you find standing alone at the end of bars. Except her eyes. They were beautiful. Even when rounded in shock they were beautiful. Brown eyes that given the chance would twinkle and dance, glow when they were looking at one special person.

"Hello, Johnny," she said, scarcely above a whisper. Her voice matched her eyes.

Now it was his turn to be stunned. Now he had a name, or part of one at least. Or that other person did, the one lurking inside, refusing to come out, amused by his discomfort and unwilling to take over for him, relieve him of the burden that was reaching the point of being intolerable.

His voice wouldn't work, not for a few seconds. Finally he managed a hoarse, strained, "Hello," and then lowered his eyes.

When he looked again she was still staring, not shocked anymore but hurt, bewildered.

Embarrassed, unsure of himself, he asked, "How are you?"

"I'm O.K.," she said, still softly, not meaning it. "How are you?"

"Fine," he lied. She had the answers for him but he was afraid to ask the questions. He knew her, too, or did he? Maybe she was just the image every man carries around with him, the girl he never really meets, the one he thinks is out there somewhere when he's young but, as the years slip away, comes to realize is only a dream. They don't make them that way, not really, so he settles for an imitation.

He was angry with himself, knew he had to do something, had to quit acting like a high school sophomore. He nodded toward the tables, said, "Would you care to sit down?" She nodded back and walked toward one near the front door, one where they would be alone, have privacy. He followed, saw that her slim, firm body was as appealing as her face.

They sat facing each other, ill at ease, neither speaking. At, last, when he was getting desperate enough to comment on the weather just to break the silence, she said, "Why, Johnny? Why did you come back? I was just getting over it, just getting better."

I guess I deserve this, he thought. It's the kind of thing you should expect when you start opening locked doors, poking around, releasing phantoms that are better left alone. He took a deep breath and began:

"Look, this may sound pretty stupid but try to understand. I don't know who I am. What I mean is, I had an accident and can't remember. I'm not the man you know, the one you think I am. I was for awhile but I'm not now." He stopped, exasperated because he couldn't better express himself. "See what I mean? I can't make myself clear, tell you what I'm trying to say so you'll understand."

She reached over and lightly touched his hand for an instant. "I understand Johnny. That's the way you used to be, only now I guess you remember things that happened before you were here the first time. Right?"

"Right," he said. "Before and after but not while I was here. Fifteen months of my life are just a blank"

"What about me?" she asked. The hurt look was back. "Do you remember me?"

Suddenly the words poured forth. He told her the story, or as much of it as he knew. When it ended he lit a cigarette, leaned toward her and said, "As for you, I remember you, I know I do, but it's still locked up somewhere in my mind." He paused, groped for words, and not finding them, shrugged and said, "To be honest, I can't remember your name. Mine either, the one you know me by."

Tears had formed in her eyes but she held them back. "I'm Lorna," she said, again barely above a whisper. "You and I, we were . . ." She hesitated, finally settled for, "We were pretty close. But Johnny, you shouldn't have come back. Not here, of all places. Something will happen, I know it will."

"Like what?"

She glanced around the room apprehensively, almost furtively. Her eyes paused when they came to the man who had bought Clary's drink, leaning now against the bar and studiously avoiding looking in their direction, and again when they reached a second man standing beside the cigarette machine near the door.

"Johnny," she said, "they're going to kill you. Not here, they'll take you somewhere else, but that's what they're going to do, I know it."

Her words hit him like a hammer. He managed a self-conscious, humorless chuckle. "What are you talking about, kill me?" he said. "Who, those men you were looking at?"

She nodded. "Arnie Martine, the one who bought you the drink, and Ange Fiocca. They work for Tony – Tony Barbano. So did you. You were one of his strong-arm men like they are. Tony's the one who found you wandering around dazed in the middle of the night along the interstate – I-90 up near Cleveland. That's how you got your name. Tony gave it to you – Johnny Ninety."

He repeated it. "Johnny Ninety. What did this Johnny Ninety do that makes you think they'll kill him?" He sounded like he was talking about someone else. He still was, in his

41

own mind.

"You ran off with nearly $200,000," she said. "You and Squints Hogan. They caught Squints, but couldn't find you. They killed him. No one's ever said so but I've overheard enough to piece it together."

"How did it happen? How did they – we – do it?"

"Tony sent you on a job. The two of you flew to Houston and were to rent a car there. I don't know the details but you were to go to Brownsville. It's on the border so I can guess what you were going to do. Anyhow, a couple of days after you left Tony was upset, furious. Ange and Arnie flew down there, were gone almost a week. They found Squints and got the money but it was too late to complete the business deal. Squints never came back. Neither did you, but I knew they didn't find you. They didn't say so but I could tell. None of them ever mentioned your name again while I was around."

"How do you know all this?"

"I'm Tony's secretary, I run his construction company office. I don't know anything about the other part of his business – the part you were in – except what I overhear. On the books you were a construction supervisor but that's not what you really were."

Thinking aloud, he said, "We must have gone to Galveston for the night for some reason. I probably went out for a walk – I like to after dinner – and got hit by a car. When I didn't come back, this Hogan decided to take off with the money. Apparently he didn't do a very good job of hiding. But if they got the money back they know I didn't take it. Why would they want to kill me?"

"They think you were in on a double-cross, you and Squints. They don't forgive something like that and you should know it, even if you can't remember."

He frowned, tried to think of a move. "Maybe," he said, "I should talk to this Tony."

"No," she said, eyes rounding in fear. "Tony looked on you as – well, almost like a son. I don't think the others ever trusted you, but Tony did. After what happened he thinks you let him down, betrayed him. Your only chance is to get out of here someway, go back to your other life, disappear again and never come back."

"If I do, what happens to you since you've been talking to me?"

She laughed a little. "I'll be O.K. Tony treats me like a daughter and thought of you as a son but he was hoping we'd get married." The thought sobered her quickly. "Are you married, Johnny?"

"No," he said, "and call me Mitch, that's my name. I was married when I was here before but didn't know it. Now I'm divorced."

"Johnny" – she had already forgotten his instructions – "you've got to get out of here. Right away."

He thought about it, agreed with her. Still, he didn't want to leave her like that. What choice was there, though? "O.K.," he said, "I think I can. You just sit quietly."

He got up, said, "Thanks," softly and walked toward the cigarette machine, fumbling in his pocket for change. The man – Ange – straightened as he approached but Clary changed directions abruptly toward the bar, took a dollar bill from his wallet and asked the bartender for change. When he got it he headed for the machine again, holding the money in his left palm and selecting the coins he wanted with his right hand.

When he reached the machine he bent over, ran his fingers along the buttons, found the right one and pressed it. The pack came tumbling down into a chute near the bottom. He reached for it with his left hand. As he straightened up he aimed a swift, unexpected punch just above Ange's belt buckle. The man gasped, doubled over and dropped to the floor. Clary bolted through the door.

Outside he stopped suddenly, jumped behind a brick facade to the left of the door. Within seconds Arnie Martine burst through the door, gun in hand, frantically looking in all directions. Before he realized where he was, Clary's knockout punch landed on his jaw. Clary sent the gun skidding over the sidewalk with his foot, sprinted across the street to his car and pulled away with tires howling in protest.

He was at the motel in less than ten minutes. He parked in the crowded lot, hurried to his room and threw the few things he had unpacked into his suitcase, went to the desk and paid his bill.

Outside again, he tossed the suitcase into the trunk, slammed the lid and climbed behind the wheel. He was fitting the key into the ignition when he felt the gun pressed against the back of his neck.

"That wasn't nice, Johnny," said a raspy voice behind him. "Running away like that just when I was ready to come in and see you after all this time. I might have missed you altogether if I got there half a minute later."

Fool, thought Clary. He hadn't glanced in the rearview mirror, not once, and hadn't thought of checking the backseat before getting into the car. He drove east again, as ordered, hands clammy, slippery on the wheel. Past the Red Arrow and then south toward the airport.

"Pull in here," said the man he knew was Tony, moving the gun slightly to the left as he spoke. It was a large, dark warehouse. Heavy equipment was parked outside and a sign read "Barbano Construction Company."

Ange and Arnie were already there, waiting in a spacious, comfortable office. Clary was patted down and pushed onto a chair in front of a large mahogany desk. Tony walked behind it, sat down and lit a cigar while the others positioned themselves behind and to each side of Clary.

Tony was smaller, better dressed, nicer looking than Clary had pictured him. He examined the cigar a minute and then looked up. "Johnny, you disappointed me," he said. "Got anything to say for yourself?"

There was no point in holding back, no point in playing coy or trying to bluff his way out. It wouldn't work, so he found himself for the second time that night repeating the story of the accidents, his loss of memory.

When he finished, Arnie Martine laughed. "Some story," he said. "Some imagination. I always said the guy was smart – too smart for his own good. I told you that you couldn't trust him, too."

"That's the way it was, Johnny?" asked Tony. Clary nodded. Several moments of silence followed and then Tony said, "Well, we've waited this long so I guess another day won't matter. We'll check it out in the morning, Johnny."

"Come on, Tony," Arnie said. "You know he's lying so let's get it over with. Even if he isn't, what could you do?

44

You can't just let him walk away, knowing what he does."

"Don't be in such a hurry, Arnie. I told you, we're going to check it out. Lock him up in the empty office and one of you guys stay here tonight." He got up and started for the door but turned and in a harsher, more commanding voice said, "And leave him alone."

The room was chilly, uncomfortable. He dozed off several times, seated in a chair, but awoke each time with a start. There was nothing to be done, the situation seemed hopeless. No wonder he had sealed the fifteen months off somewhere in the back of his mind. A hired tough, probably even a drug runner and God knows what else. The girl, Lorna, was the only good part. She was special. Different than anyone he had known.

It was mid-morning when he heard her voice. "Johnny. Can you hear me, Johnny?" Soft, muffled. He couldn't pinpoint where it was coming from, thought for a minute he was imagining it. "Johnny, Johnny," again, just above a whisper. It wasn't imagination, it was real and coming from a cold-air register near the floor.

"Yes," he said, crouching in front of it, "I hear you."

"Listen, I've only got a minute. I've got a key, one they've forgotten about. When Tony goes to lunch, one of them will go with him. The other should be up front in the offices. I'll unlock the door and you be ready to go, but don't talk, just follow me. My car's outside."

"Then what? Where do you think we can go?"

"We'll worry about that after we get away from here. I have to go now, so you be ready. "

It would be crazy, he knew. Okay for him, he had nothing to lose, but too risky for her. They'd be after her as much as they'd be after him. It wasn't fair, not to her. It did offer hope, though, and that's more than he had now. Still he wasn't sure, didn't know what he'd do when she unlocked the door.

He needn't have worried. When the door opened at eleven-thirty it was Arnie. "Come on," he said, "Tony wants to see you." He was angry and it was more than the anger he'd feel because of the unexpected punch, the humiliation it caused.

Clary was led back to the plush office. Ange was waiting by the door, but Tony dismissed them both. "Wait up front," he said. "Go do something for a while."

"Tony —" Arnie began but he was cut off by a terse command to "Go!"

When they were alone Tony said, "Well, Johnny, your story checks. All of it. The hospital in Galveston, the things in Albany before and after you were here, everything."

He had known it would, of course, if anyone took the time to investigate. That wasn't the issue. The important thing was what Tony planned now. Arnie was right; he knew too much. He might not remember it now, but they couldn't be sure of that and there also was always the chance it would come back to him in the future.

"O.K.," Clary said, "where do we go from here?"

Tony unwrapped a cigar, smiled and said, "That's up to you, Johnny. Want your old job back?"

Clary laughed wryly. "I'm no hood, Tony," he said, "no matter what I did when I was here before."

Tony put his head back, laughed, too. "Don't use such harsh words, Johnny. How about saying businessman? You were a businessman yourself."

"Not this kind of business, Tony, not your kind. So what happens if I say no?"

"You walk out the door."

"Just like that? No strings attached? What if I remember, what if it comes back to me. What's to keep me from turning you in?"

"You won't," Tony said. "Believe me, I've thought about it and what's to turn in? It'd be your word against that of a respected businessman. Besides, you don't know much anyway."

"You mean I can get up and walk out now?"

"Right," Tony said, leaning forward and lowering his voice. "But before you do, consider this. I like you, Johnny, I always have. You've got a lot on the ball and I need a number-two man, need one bad. Arnie and Ange are good boys, but not the executive type, know what I mean?"

Clary nodded.

"So," Tony continued, "what would you say to fifty thou a year? Plus, if you and Lorna decide to tie the knot, the deed to that nice place I own out past the lake in the country. Call it a little wedding present."

Clary was surprised by the offer. "What would I do for that fifty thou?"

"We'll be starting on a new shopping mall down near Canton when the weather breaks. You'd be kind of an overseer, make sure everything goes okay. Nothing to it." He paused, smiled and added, "Of course there'll be other things from time to time."

Clary shook his head. "No thanks, that's not for me. So can I leave now? I'm hungry, dirty and tired."

Tony raised his eyebrows, shrugged his shoulders. "If that's what you want, Johnny. I told you, it's up to you."

"Thanks for the offer," Clary said, standing up and walking to the door. "See you around, maybe."

Tony nodded and Clary walked out.

Lorna, tense, pale, looked at him as he approached her desk. "Ange told me," she said. "I can't believe Tony's just going to let you go like that."

"It surprised me, too," he said, grinning, "but he is. It's lunch time, can you get away?"

She nodded, got up and walked with him to the door. They drove in his car to the Red Arrow, sat at the same table, ordered sandwiches.

"Well, Johnny . . ." she began, but he interrupted.

"Mitch, remember?"

She smiled, shook her head. "I guess you'll always be Johnny to me. Anyway, what are you going to do, go back to being a salesman?"

"Manufacturer's representative," he corrected.

They sat without speaking for a few minutes. He wanted her, wanted her with him. Eighteen hours earlier he hadn't known she existed. Now it seemed like he'd always known her. Maybe he had, in his mind. In his dreams. Now that she had materialized, was alive and real, he didn't want to walk away from her. He wouldn't find her again, he knew that.

"Want to come with me?" he asked abruptly, almost brusquely.

She looked into his eyes and said, "Do you want me to?"

He nodded.

47

"What would I do?" she said. "In a strange place and with you traveling so much?"

He hadn't had time to think about that. What would it be like for her? Is a wildflower ever the same after it's uprooted and left alone in alien surroundings? He didn't know. And money, what about that? He was getting by but he'd want more than that for her. She should have the best, that's all he could visualize for her. Not some small apartment in a strange city, always pinching pennies, alone most of the time. No, she should have the best. That took money. Lots of money. With money you could have the things you wanted, do the things you wanted to do. Nothing else would be satisfactory. Not for her, not in *his* mind.

The door opened, jarring him from his reverie. Tony walked in, flanked by Ange and Arnie. Tony raised his hand a few inches, wiggled the fingers and winked.

"I never thought they'd let you go," she repeated softly.

"He's not a bad guy."

"I know he isn't, not the way you mean it. No one could be nicer to me. But in the other way, the other part of his business . . . well, you know."

She was unaware of Tony's offer. Money, lots of it. A luxurious place to live. Second in command, head man someday. It was tainted money, of course, but that's what she was paid with every Friday. It spent just like the other kind, too. Besides, when you come right down to it how much of the stuff is lily-white?

He stood up, startling her with the suddenness of the move. She looked up at him and said, "Where are you going?"

"Have to see Tony a minute."

He went to the table where the three men were eating, stooped and said something to Tony. He got up and the two of them walked to the end of the bar where they had privacy. They talked quietly a few minutes, shook hands and returned to their tables.

"What was that all about?" she asked. Then, after a pause, added, "Mitch."

He looked around, pretending to be puzzled. "Who're you talking to?" he said, starting to grin. "Something wrong with your memory? My name's Johnny – Johnny Ninety."

TICKETS FOR THE GAME

I was drinking coffee at the diner out on the bypass, thinking how warm it was for mid-November and wishing I had tickets for the big game that afternoon. It was out of the question, though. Both Purdue and Indiana had had good seasons so tickets were scarce and the only way to get into Ross-Ade Stadium was to pay scalpers' prices. That's why it was out of the question as far as I was concerned.

I was on the end stool, the one just before the curve in the counter. A weary looking man, red-eyed and unshaven, came in and took the first stool beyond the curve so we were sitting half facing each other. He ordered coffee, too, and while waiting for it he took a narrow envelope from his pocket and began tapping it on the counter.

The Purdue logo was on the upper left corner and I knew by the shape that it contained tickets for the game. I looked up from it to his face, wondered about his haggard appearance and decided he must have arrived the night before and indulged in a little too much pre-game hilarity.

That's one of the ironies of life, a lot of people inside any football stadium have so much under their belts they don't know what's happening down on the field, while outside are thousands of guys like me who would give their eyeteeth to see the game.

He turned his head a little and caught me staring at him. Maybe he had seen me looking at the envelope earlier because he said, "Could you use a couple of tickets to the game today?"

The question was unexpected and I had to grope around for the right answer. Sure, I could use them. The problem was I couldn't pay for them. It must have been written all over my face because he said, "They're yours for the taking if you want them. No charge, I'm not going to be using them."

I was thrilled, naturally, but at the same time a little embarrassed so I said, "Gee, I really appreciate it," and it came out sounding like something a high school kid would say after asking for his first date and being accepted.

His coffee had arrived by then and be sipped it, staring over the top of his cup with a far-away look. When he put it down he said, "It'll be the first IU-Purdue game I've missed since the war."

I still had that uneasy, self-conscious feeling you get when a stranger gives you something that way so the high school kid was talking again when I said, "Gosh, that's too bad. If you think there's some way you might get out –"

He shook me off. "No, I won't be using them. You see, Ginny – that's my wife – and I were going like we always do. I was going to meet her here in Lafayette this morning but —" his voice trailed off and he picked up his cup again. I didn't say anything so after a few seconds he went on:

"Ginny and I got married right after I got back from the war. We met at IU and seemed to hit it off right away. That would have been the fall of 'forty-two because I went in the army the following summer. She waited for me, though. I knew she would; she wasn't one of those out-of-sight-out-of-mind kind of girls.

"That was funny, too, because I've never been much to look at but Ginny's always been a knockout. Never lost her looks. Guys ten, even fifteen years younger always have had an eye for her, but she' s been a one-man woman.

"That last night before I left for the army we sat up all night on a bench there on campus, We didn't say much – hell, there wasn't much you *could* say – but along toward morning when it first started to get light off in the east I told her to go ahead and have fun and if somebody else came along, well, not to worry about me.

"She cut me off, put a finger on my lips and said, 'I told you I'll be waiting. Now hush.'"

He looked at me then, so I nodded my head to show I'd been listening, and said, "You were lucky, A lot of them said that but didn't mean it."

He smiled kind of to himself and drank more coffee. "That's right," he said, "I was lucky. I've always known that, believe me."

I was still ill at ease, wondering what he was leading up to, sort of expecting it to be that she had been in an accident or something like that. He was lost in thought for a minute or two, but then looked at me and said, "You don't mind my talking to you, do you?"

What could I say? It was bothering me, sure, but you don't accept a favor from someone and then turn around and be rude. I shook my head and said, "No, of course not."

He smiled to himself again, lit a cigarette and said, "We've never been like some married couples, each going their own way, know what I mean? Ginny and I have always done things together like football games, things like that. You know how some women are, never interested in the same thing their husband is. Not Ginny, she's always wanted to go along, no matter where I was going.

"Maybe that's because she's always been alone a lot. I'm a salesman, usually leave on Monday morning and don't get home again until Friday night. We don't have kids; Ginny always wanted them, but she had a miscarriage the year after we were married and the doctor told her that was it. Neither one of us has much in the way of a family, either, so she's had to spend a lot of time by herself. I suppose that's made us even closer, is one reason it's always been so great that we get along like we have.

"I know it's been tough on her, having me on the road so much. We've got a nice big yard, though – we live just outside of Indianapolis – and she enjoys working around the place when the weather's good, and then in winter she reads a lot. I always call home either Tuesday or Wednesday night and we talk for fifteen, twenty minutes. Sometimes half an hour. It gets a little expensive, but it breaks up the week, makes it go by a lot faster."

I realized he was talking about her in the present tense and figured I had been wrong and maybe she was just sick or something. I was hoping so for his sake, and mine, too. It's funny how sometimes you know a person just wants to talk, but it isn't really you he's talking to, you just happen to be there. It's awkward, hearing intimate things about someone else's life that you don't want to hear, but have no choice. I don't handle situations like that too well. The only thing I can think of to do is try to change the subject, but they always go right back to it.

He nodded his head and said, "Yeah, Ginny's been looking forward to it but –" He lit another cigarette, finished his coffee and went on, "I was working up along the lake this week. Started in Sheboygan on Monday and worked my way back through Milwaukee and Racine. Then next Monday I'd go back up to Kenosha and work down to Chicago. Anyway, we decided that since I'd have to go right by Lafayette on my way home it would be fun to make a long weekend of it and meet here last night.

"I made reservations at the motel across the street for Friday, Saturday and Sunday nights. That way Ginny could drive up, bring me fresh clothes for next week, and we could have a few drinks Friday night, take in the game on Saturday and then just relax, do whatever we felt like on Sunday. Monday morning I'd start out from here and Ginny would drive back home.

"Well, wouldn't that of all weeks it would be this one when I got tied up with a good customer and was going to have to see again the first thing this morning when his partner would be back in town and could okay a contract. That hasn't happened in years. Anyway, it would still give me time to get down here for the game so I called Ginny at noon yesterday and told her how things stood, but to come up just like we planned and I'd meet her as soon as I could get away.

"Well, it turned out the partner took a Friday evening flight, so the three of us got together at the airport at nine o'clock and had everything taken care of in a few minutes. On the way back to the motel I decided to drive on down right away instead of waiting till morning so I checked out and was on my way before ten.

"It was late when I got here, of course, so I went to the desk, found out what room Ginny was in and got a key. I guess she had been over in the lounge and had one too many. Anyway, she was asleep like I knew she would be. Kind of passed out, really."

He stopped talking, lit another cigarette and stared off into space. That went on for a few minutes and I would just as soon have gotten up and walked away, but knew I couldn't do that. Finally, figuring it was best to get it over with, I said, "Was anything wrong?"

He gave me a real funny look and then kind of smiled a little. "Yeah," he said at last. "There was a guy with her. A young guy, probably about thirty. Like I said, she had way too much to drink and I don't know if she even knew the guy was there. Besides, I guess it wasn't right, walking in on her that way, but I never thought a thing about it."

There was a long silence, one of those you have to experience yourself because it can't be described. I just stared down at my empty cup, and I could tell he was looking straight ahead, probably not even aware I was still there.

It seemed like that silence lasted for hours. It really might have if it depended on me to make the first move, but suddenly he sort of jerked, dropped the envelope in front of me, laid his hand on my arm and said, "Well, I have to be getting back. Hope you enjoy the game."

I wanted to thank him again, but by the time I could get my tongue untied he was on his way out the door. I turned and watched him go, but he only went as far as the phone booth out by the highway. It was a long call, must have lasted at least five minutes. When he finally hung up he went on across the road and into one of the ground-level rooms at the motel. I guess I was curious by then because I ordered another cup of coffee and switched over to the stool where he had been sitting so I could look out the window without having to turn around.

After a few minutes a police car pulled into the motel lot. I had a real funny feeling, almost like l was sick, when I saw it.

The two policemen just had time to get out when another cruiser arrived and then an unmarked car with two men in street clothes who you could pick out a mile away as detectives.

One of the men in uniform tried the door that the man who gave me the tickets had gone in not more than five minutes earlier. It wouldn't open, so he kind of trotted down to the office and came back with a key. They all went inside but, after a minute or so three of the men in uniform came out and two of then drove away in one of the cruisers. The other stayed by the door.

A few more minutes went by and then another unmarked car pulled up and the two detectives in it went inside carrying a camera and some other equipment. Then another man arrived, one with a black bag like doctors used to carry when they made house calls.

Nothing more happened for about fifteen minutes, then an ambulance came and right behind it was a second one. By then a crowd had gathered and people in the diner were standing up looking out. I really felt sick, didn't want to look any more, but couldn't help myself.

I guess someone was standing in front of me when the ambulance crews went inside because I didn't see them. Pretty soon two men came out carrying a stretcher that was covered with a sheet. Then the second crew also came out carrying a covered stretcher. In the meantime the first two men had gone back inside and before long they came back with another load. That made three, Ginny, her husband and the other man. Which had been which? I wondered.

I sat there for quite awhile, feeling pretty bad, kind of blaming myself about the man. When he talked to me it would have been too late to do anything about the others, but I couldn't shake the idea that I should have helped him some way. Finally I realized that was crazy. I had no idea what he had already done so how could I have guessed what he planned to do when he got back to the motel?

When I looked at my watch it was getting on toward noon so I got up and went out to the phone booth, the same one the man had used to call the police. That got me wondering how he had done it, knowing they would get there within a few minutes. I pushed the thought out of my mind because I really didn't want to know.

I started to dial Bill's number since we always go to games together, but hung up halfway through and started over, only this time dialing my own number. When my wife answered I said, "Honey, get your jacket and wait at the door for me. I'll pick you up in a few minutes, we're going to the game."

She was kind of surprised. It was the first one I had taken her to for a long time. It was silly, I suppose, but I thought the man would have liked that. I did, too.

STRANGE, BUT TRUE

The only time the celebrated French attorney, Paree Maison, lost a case was when a ship on which he was a passenger struck an iceberg in the North Sea. "I had a case of champagne on board," Maison told reporters later, "and I lost it."

One of the foreign reporters, a former Nazi with no sense of humor and a violent temper, was so incensed by the remark he immediately assaulted the attorney, cracking forty or fifty of his victim's bones before being pulled off.

When the reporter went to trial, Maison left his hospital bed and volunteered to defend the man, since no competent lawyer wished to take the case. Maison's was a pitiful figure as he hobbled around the courtroom in his splints and bandages, eloquently arguing for compassion for the defendant. Despite his pleas, however, the jury brought in a verdict of guilty, and the offender was sentenced to twenty years at hard labor on Devil's Island.

When someone pointed out that this was a case he did not win, Paree Maison smiled enigmatically and said, "But what makes you think I lost?"

Fillers in Mike Shayne Mystery Magazine sometimes were items of droll humor such as this.

A BLEND OF MURDER

Jablonski placed the pack of tobacco on the counter at the same time Mervin Darcy said, "Better make it two."

Not much of an inconvenience, a few steps down the aisle again, but still it was typical of Mervin Darcy. The expression on Darcy's face told Stanley Jablonski the man had known all along that he wanted two packs. Giving orders, making those he dealt with fetch and carry, was one of life's pleasures for Mervin Darcy. Keeping people off balance, never letting them know what to expect, was another. He packed weight and enjoyed throwing it around.

Jablonski mumbled his thanks when a dollar bill and the correct number of coins were dropped on the counter. He busied himself at the cash register as the smirking, florid-faced Darcy walked out the door. No more than ten seconds passed before it was flung open again and Garland Gant, owner of the jewelry store next door, burst wild-eyed into the Leatherstocking Pipe Shop.

"That s.o.b." Gant shouted. "I could kill him!"

Jablonski chuckled. "Talking about Mervin Darcy, I suppose."

"You know I am, Jab, who else? You'll never believe what he's done this time."

Jablonski, resuming his polishing of a stubby, curved Jobey, shrugged his shoulders and said, "Maybe not, but try me."

57

"Remember about three months ago he bought an engagement ring? The best I had in the store. Paid nearly two thousand for it."

Jablonski nodded. "Never could figure what Jenny Palmer sees in the guy unless it's money."

"Whatever it was, it's over. Just before he came in here Darcy was in the store and said the engagement's off and demanded his money back. All of it, can you imagine?"

Jablonski gave the Jobey a final loving swipe with the polishing cloth before placing it in a display case. "Knowing Darcy I can. Wonder what happened, though. Whatever it was, you can bet Darcy was the cause of it."

"I hear he's been escorting Hazel Miniver around lately. That wouldn't have set well with Jenny, them being engaged and all."

"S'pect not. Far as the money goes, don't see you're obligated to refund it after all this time."

"What can I do?" Gant said, palms extended, facial muscles sagging. "He's one of my best customers and he knows it. I started to write out a check but he said he wanted cash so I told him I'd get it when the banks open in the morning."

"Up to you, Garland. Lot of money, though. Not sure what I'd do under the circumstances, good customer or not."

It was still on Jablonski's mind half an hour later when he locked up and walked down Main Street to the Veteran's Club, coat collar turned up against a biting north wind off Otsego Lake. A drink and a little conversation at the club, dinner at the hotel around the corner, an evening with a good book in front of the wood stove at home. The cold weather rut that Jablonski loved. There was no room for the likes of Mervin Darcy in the comfortable routine so he pushed the thoughts aside.

The ringing of the telephone, disturbingly loud at nine in the morning, startled Jablonski. "First time the damn thing's rung in a week," he complained aloud although he was alone in the shop. "Hell of a way to start the day, talking on the telephone." He picked it up and snarled, "Lo," into the mouthpiece.

"Can you get away from the shop for a little while, Jab, and come down to Mervin Darcy's place on Lake Street?"

58

Jablonski recognized the caller's voice, realized it contained a note of urgency, but still he hesitated. The fact Hubert Turner was chief of police didn't give him the right to expect people to close up shop and come running at his beck and call.

"Don't know, Hubert. Means I'd have to lock up and — "

"It's important, Jab, or I wouldn't ask."

The first coffee of the day was starting to run from the machine down into the glass server and Jablonski studied the stream of dark liquid longingly. Damn, he thought but aloud said, "All right, Hubert, all right. So close I'll just walk down. Be there in five minutes."

Jablonski grudgingly unplugged the coffee maker, hung a sign promising his imminent return in the window, locked the door and set out, muttering aloud over the lack of consideration shown by public employees. "Think a businessman can just walk out any time he feels like it, customers and money be damned." The only living thing within hearing, a small, wiry-haired black dog shivering in the doorway of Gant's Jewelry Store, responded with a feeble wag of its tail.

The nearly deserted street indicated few customers would be inconvenienced by Jablonski's absence and his coffee would suffer little loss. He'd sell some tobacco and a few cigars later in the day, perhaps even a pipe or two. For the most part, however, the tourists who provided the bulk of his business had abandoned Cooperstown for the winter. There'd be a scattering of them visiting the Baseball Hall of Fame a block down the street and some out at the Farmers Museum, but aside from the two weeks preceding Christmas he'd keep the shop open the next few months more as a service to regular customers than as a money-making proposition.

As he turned onto Pioneer Street the wind off the lake two blocks away stung his cheeks, made him lean forward to maintain his balance. Whitecaps crowned the choppy gray water and, Jablonski thought, if Fenimore Cooper could see the lake today he certainly wouldn't call it the Glimmerglass.

Hubert Turner held the front door open as Jablonski approached Mervin Darcy's large white house. Like many of the older ones in the village it was set back from the sidewalk only enough to allow the opening of the door without endangering

59

passersby. Jablonski pushed his way past Turner and the chief, battling the wind, closed the door behind him. In a muted voice the heavy-set, uniformed man, perspiring despite the chill in the air, said, "Do you know what happened?"

"Yep. You asked me to close up shop and come down —"

"No, no, Jab. I mean about Darcy?"

Jablonski studied the other man from dark eyes under bushy gray brows that now were raised. The chief, he thought, needed exercise. Like vigorously pushing himself away from the dinner table. He said, "What about Darcy? And why the hell are you whispering?"

The chief cleared his throat and, after a false start, said self-consciously and too loudly, "He's dead."

"Dead? I'll be damned!" Jablonski paused, let the surprising news sink in. Then, more subdued, "Why call me, Hubert? Mervin and I weren't exactly bosom buddies."

"You sell him tobacco, don't you?"

"Did. Lost a customer, though, from the sound of it. Right at the start of the slow season, too."

"You can tell one kind of tobacco from another, can't you?"

"Raw tobaccos or blends?"

"The kind you sell at the shop."

Jablonski sighed. People could be so damned stupid. "Blends," he said softly and then, louder, "My God, Hubert, have you any idea how many of them there are? Hundreds, literally hundreds." He shook his head, gritted his teeth, let his shoulders sag. "Is that what you got me down here for, to try to identify a blend?"

Turner gave him a crestfallen look and a hangdog nod.

Jablonski's eyebrows went up again as the implication of the chief's summons finally dawned on him. He said, "Suppose you tell me what's going on, Hubert. You trying to say Mervin Darcy's been murdered?"

Turner stepped up the tempo of his nodding. "Murder or suicide."

"Humph!" Jablonski countered the chief's nodding by emphatically shaking his own head from side to side. "Not suicide," he asserted. "Not Mervin Darcy. Too sold on himself for that. Besides, he bought two packs of tobacco just yesterday

60

afternoon."

Bewilderment showed in Turner's face. "What's that got to do with it?"

"Hubert, why in the hell would he buy two packs if he was getting set to do himself in?"

"Maybe he just decided sudden like."

"Mervin Darcy? Ridiculous! But are we going to stand here all morning, Hubert, or are you going to show me that tobacco?"

"In here," Turner said, walking a few steps down the hall and turning into a large room lined on all four sides by ceiling-high bookshelves. Jablonski followed but once inside the room stopped short, startled by the sight of Darcy's lifeless body seated with legs crossed in a high-backed leather chair. A pistol was gripped in his right hand and the front of his smoking jacket was crusted with dried blood. An expensive Dunhill briar lay in his lap.

"Damn it, Hubert," Jablonski complained, "you might have warned me he was sitting here like this. Gave me a start, coming on him that way."

"Sorry, Jab. Guess I forgot."

"Forgot?" Jablonski, shaking his head, chuckled a little. "Tell me, Hubert, how many murders you handled?"

"Not too many."

"How many?"

"One, I guess,"

"This one, right?"

Turner nodded sheepishly. "Don't get too many here."

"Good thing, I'd say. Hate to have you forget and leave bodies sitting all over town. As long as you had to have one, though, it don't surprise me any it's Darcy. Any man that'd treat a pipe the way he did —"

"How's that, Jab?"

"Banging them against anything handy to knock the ashes out. Letting the cake build up until it was thicker than the bowl."

"That's bad, is it?"

"Course it's bad. Always scarring them up or breaking them. And letting the cake get so thick is what cracks the bowl. Heat expansion. Really burns me up to see somebody mistreat a good pipe."

Jablonski scowled when he caught Turner studying him. "You can quit giving me the fish eye, Hubert. I didn't shoot him just because he was a pipe abuser, if that's what you're thinking."

"Course not, Jab. I wasn't thinking anything like that. It's just that you sounded so — "

Turner anxious to change the subject, walked with exaggerated briskness to a table beside a chair facing the one holding the body and ten feet or so from it. Pointing to a large glass ashtray he said, "Here's the tobacco."

Jablonski joined him, knelt beside the table and examined the contents of the ashtray. It held a quantity of ashes, half a dozen cigarette butts and what appeared to be nearly a full bowl of unburned pipe tobacco. He picked up a little of the tobacco peered at it closely for a moment and said, "Well, this isn't Darcy's. I can tell you that straight off."

"You recognize it, Jab? "

"Yep. One of my own blends as a matter of fact. Blend 15, the one I call Mohican. A treat for the outdoorsman."

"Why do you call it that, Jab?"

"Cause if you smoke it inside, most women would boot you right out of the house. It's strong. Pretty heady stuff." Jablonski's upper body rocked in silent laughter. "Figured Mohican was a good name for it. If the tribe had used this blend in their peace pipes it might have been the last of them. "

Turner's face was blank for a moment, then he grinned. "I get it, Jab. Last of the Mohicans, right?"

Jablonski muttered something unintelligible under his breath, sighed and said, "Right, Hubert, you figured it out."

"How do you know for sure that's what it is?"

"By the Irish Aromatic. Only use it in two blends and Blend 10 -- Sultan of Swat – only has two percent of it. Mohican has eighteen percent and besides it has perique and latakia and Blend 10 doesn't."

"How many guys smoke this Mohican?"

"Not many. Half a dozen regulars, maybe. Sell a lot to tourists, though."

"The regulars, is Leo Stack one of em?"

Jablonski frowned, pursed his lips. "How'd you know that, Hubert?" There was a note of surprise, even something bordering on respect, in his voice.

The chief drew himself up to his full height, looked over both shoulders conspiratorially, and lowering his voice said, "Don't know if I should tell you this or not, Jab, but Leo Stack and Darcy had been having their troubles lately."

"Humph! Everybody in town knows that, Hubert, it's not some big secret. Problem over that land deal they went in on together up at the north end of the lake. Now don't tell me from just that and this here tobacco you've got Leo Stack pegged as the murderer?"

"More than that," Turner said defensively. "Leo, or somebody who looked a lot like him, was seen leaving here about ten last night. Madder'n hell and in a hurry, too."

"That's it? No real evidence? Humph!"

"Don't make light of it, Jab," Turner said aggrievedly; "I've got it all figured out. Just needed you to identify the tobacco to be sure it really was Leo who was here."

"What about those cigarette butts? Looks to me like some-body else was here, too."

The chief's head wagged back and forth. "Nope. Everybody knows Leo smokes cigarettes, too, not just a pipe."

"Well you're right about that much, at least," Jablonski ad-mitted.

Smugly, Turner said, "Way I figure it, Leo started out smoking his pipe but got all excited and switched to cigarettes. That's why hardly any of the pipe tobacco is burned. Left his cigarettes and matches there on the table, too, when he rushed out."

Jablonski bent over again and examined the book of paper matches. The cover, imprinted with the name of Stack's real estate firm, had been left open and half of the matches were missing.

"Don't touch 'em, Jab," Turner cautioned.

"Think I'm that stupid?" Jablonski snapped. He took a pipe nail from his pocket and used it to carefully turn over each butt in the ashtray. After a moment or two he said, "Humph!" Satisfied, he straightened up, flexed his legs several times and asked:

"Where'd the gun come from, Hubert?"

"It's Darcy's. Old Minnie, his housekeeper – she found the body when she came in this morning – says he kept it in that desk over there."

"That why you thought it might be suicide?"

"That and the gun being in his hand, but I never really thought he did it himself. Leo stuck the gun in his hand to make it look that way. Didn't fool me at all."

"How you figure Leo knew the gun was in the desk?"

The chief shrugged his shoulders. "Probably saw it sometime when Darcy opened the drawer."

"So what now? Going to arrest, Leo?"

"Yep. I'd like to have it wrapped up before I call in the state police. Course I'll let Leo tell his side of it if he wants to."

"That might be a good idea," Jablonski said sarcastically. Without the sarcasm he asked, "Going to arrest whoever else was here last night, too?"

"You talking about those butts again, Jab? I told you, everybody knows Leo smokes cigarettes."

"Everybody see him wearing lipstick while he smoked one?"

Turner, puzzled, said, "What are you talking about?"

"Take a close look. One of those butts has a trace of lipstick on it."

The chief knelt beside the table, his nose an inch from the ashtray. "Well I'll be darned," he said. "It looks like lipstick, all right. Just a touch, didn't notice it before."

"Now look at the matches."

Turner moved his head, squinted at the matches, finally said, "What about 'em?"

Jablonski shook his head in aggravation. "Look close, Hubert. Look how they're torn out. It's the oldest twist in detective stories, you read about it all the time. Half are torn off the right side but one's torn off the left."

The chief turned back to the matches and murmured, nodding his head at the same time, "Yeah, I see what you mean. One must have been pulled out by a left-handed person."

"Right Hubert, and one cigarette was smoked by a woman. Seems like a reasonable assumption that a left-handed woman smoked the last cigarette."

Turner, with several grunts and a long groan, got back on his feet. Scratching the back of his head he said, "I hear Mervin broke up with Jenny Palmer. Guess I'd better talk to her, too."

Jablonski walked to the desk, pulled out the chair and sat down front-to-rear so his legs straddled the back. "Sit down a minute, Hubert," he said, "and let's talk about it."

Turner hesitated a moment before easing his bulky frame into a chair well away from the body. "Okay, Jab," he said without enthusiasm. "Seems to me this is kind of out of your line, though."

"That makes two of us, then. But anyway, Hubert, a lot of people besides Leo Stack didn't care too much for old Mervin there, me included. Like you say, there was Jenny because of the engagement. Garland Gant, too. Just yesterday Mervin demands a full refund on the ring he bought months ago. Then there's Hazel Miniver."

"Hazel Miniver? How's she fit in?"

"Hear she and Mervin had been going together. Maybe she was expecting that ring when he got it back from Jenny."

Turner shook his head. "Jenny seems more likely to me. Understand she took off the ring and threw it at Mervin when she ran into him at the country club. Maybe she came down here last night to try to make up with him. Probably knew where he kept the gun so when it didn't work out, she got it and shot him."

"Not likely," Jablonski argued. "Too proud to come begging. Besides, Mervin would have been on guard, knowing her temper and all. Look how relaxed he was sitting there, legs crossed, smoking his pipe. Same thing if it had been Leo. If they were really having it out, Mervin wouldn't have been so easy in his mind. Especially if Leo, or Jenny for that matter, was fooling around over at the desk where the gun was."

"I don't know, Jab," Turner said doubtfully.

"Now Hubert, you know how Mervin liked to play cat and mouse with people. Always playing the role of the big man. Maybe he led Hazel Miniver on, let her think she was going to get that ring. Can't you imagine how she'd have looked forward to showing it around, lording it over Jenny? So suppose she came here expecting to get it and then found out he'd taken it back to the store. Probably knew where the gun was kept, too. Mervin was just sitting there enjoying himself, watching her stew, so finally she blew her stack, pulled out the gun before he realized what she was doing and shot him. Then she panicked, stuck the gun in his hand and ran out."

The chief sat quietly, his face blank, eyes fixed on the books across the room. Several minutes passed before he returned to Jablonski and said, "Could be, I guess. Maybe I'd better talk to Hazel first of all."

"Good idea, Hubert. Be interesting to see if she's left-handed. State police might match up the lipstick, too. Course I could be wrong, but it's worth looking into, I'd say."

Jablonski was hanging up his coat after returning from lunch when the chief entered the shop. Turner had changed from baggy trousers and a frayed jacket into his best uniform. He swaggered past the counter, chest out, stomach in. Jablonski stared at him, frowning. The man seemed transformed, a confident figure of authority.

"Thought you should be the first to know, Jab," he said. "We were dead right. Hazel Miniver broke down two minutes after I got to her place. Admitted everything. Happened just the way we figured except the gun was already out on top of the desk. Mervin and Leo must have really been having it out before she got there and Mervin finally ran him off with the gun". Hazel said she wouldn't have known it was there otherwise."

"Is she left-handed?" Jablonski asked.

"Forgot to find out. I'll do that, though. I called in the boys from the state to wrap things up. It makes me look pretty good, having Hazel in jail before I brought them into it. I might not have been able to do it as quick as I did without your help, Jab, so I wanted to thank you."

"Humph!" Jablonski took the pipe from his mouth, banged it roughly against the edge of a metal ashtray in the manner of Mervin Darcy.

"Nothing to thank me for, Hubert. Just protecting my business. Lost one regular customer thanks to this mess so I wasn't about to let you lock up Leo Stack and take another away from me. No sir, not right at the start of the slow season."

GOOD ODDS FOR MURDER

"You're going on secret, Ferg."

Foley uncrossed his legs, leaned forward and stared in disbelief at the man on the other side of the desk. "Secret? I haven't worked undercover in five years. What's the deal?"

"We've got a problem out at Kirklin Truck Company. Heard anything about it?"

" Only that we've had people out there."

"Six people," said Casey, leaning back in his swivel chair and tapping the ends of his fingers together. "Six people without any real results."

"Who'd you send, the Boy Scouts?"

"Most of them have been green, but we've had a couple of experienced men in the plant, guys who should've gotten the job done. That's why we're sending you. We need the best man we've got out there."

Foley curled one side of his mouth contemptuously. "Cut the soft soap, Casey. What's the assignment?"

"It's simple," replied the burly, raspy-voiced manager of Wellington's National Detective Agency. Branches in thirty-five principal cities and half a dozen foreign countries. "Lay a few bets on the horses, that's all you'll have to do."

Foley sat back and recrossed his legs, incredulity showing again in his face. "You mean that's it? You've had six men at Kirklin on a thing like that and none of them's done any good?"

"Right. Apparently it's not as easy as it sounds, but I can't believe it's that well-hidden an operation because Digger Brown's outfit is taking ten thousand bucks a week out of the plant."

Foley shifted his gaze to the window, contemplated the steeple towering seven stories above the cathedral next door for a moment and then asked, "So what's Kirklin's angle? Don't try to tell me the company gives a damn how much organized crime takes from the workers as long as it doesn't affect corporate profits."

Casey, relieved that selling the assignment to the headstrong Foley wasn't proving as difficult as he anticipated, propped his feet up on the mahogany desk, loosened his necktie and chuckled.

"Right again, Ferg," he said. "The company couldn't care less if the employees want to drop every cent they earn making wagers on tomorrow's price of tea in Pago Pago, but the wives have been raising hell. Kirklin's been getting so many phone calls and visits from irate women complaining that the old man arrives home minus half his pay that it's become a damn nuisance."

Foley shook his head, his face twisting in a sneer. "The heartwarming concern of big business for the working class."

"Knock it off, Ferg," Casey said, waving toward the door in a gesture of dismissal. "We just do the job, we don't analyze the client's motive. Go see Hudson; he'll fill you in on the details."

Foley tapped his fingers on the frosted glass of the door next to Casey's office, walked in without waiting for a response and said, "So what do I need to know before I head out to Kirklin?"

"You're going, are you?" answered the starchy, bespectacled man behind the desk bearing a *Neal Hudson Assistant Manager* nameplate.

"I work here, don't I? Casey says 'go,' I go."

"I've got everything ready for you. We'll start with a film."

"Might have known," Foley mumbled and then, louder, "Who's playing the lead, Clint Eastwood or Steve McQueen?"

Hudson wasn't amused. Hudson seldom was amused by Foley's barracks humor, and the antagonism between the two dripped from his voice as he said, "This is serious business, Foley, even though it may not seem so to you."

" Save the preaching for Sunday, will you? Just lay it out for me."

Hudson opened his mouth to reply, thought better of it, drew the drapes, flipped on the projector and cut the lights. The film began without the running commentary he had planned to go with it.

The first scene was taken from a second-story window overlooking the main intersection near the Kirklin plant. A brick wall surrounding the ancient buildings was visible on the left and across the street was a tavern with doors opening at an angle on the corner. Next to it was a jewelry store with a large clock suspended above the sidewalk.

When the clock showed high noon, a large black sedan turned the corner at the same time a man carrying a briefcase stepped from the tavern. The timing was so precise that the car didn't make a complete stop as the man passed the briefcase through the window.

"That was on a Tuesday," Hudson said.

"Let me guess," said Foley. "That was the bagman handing over the receipts."

Hudson's lips pursed and he remained silent until the scene was repeated and he said, "Wednesday."

"What d'ya wanna bet this is Thursday?" said Foley when it came on again. The rest of the week passed in silence.

Next came several views of another man entering or leaving a different tavern, one almost directly beneath the room where the first scenes had been shot. "Mike Kravich," Hudson said. "He owns the tavern and also is a foreman at Kirklin. He heads up the in-plant operation for Digger Brown's organization."

The end of the film flapped wildly on the reel as Hudson cut the switch and opened the drapes. "Aw, shucks," Foley said, "no cartoon."

Hudson, mustering his frostiest, most formal tone, said, "Just place some bets on the horses. Forget the numbers, everyone who has gone out has scored on them."

" So I make a few bets, then what?"

"You'll be pulled out. The company will confront those involved with the evidence we've gathered and they'll be fired. The union won't try to back them up on something like this."

Foley chuckled. "After that I suppose Digger Brown and his boys'll pack their suitcases and slink away in the night."

"They'll get back in, of course," Hudson snapped, "But their operation will be disrupted for awhile and Kirklin will have something to tell the wives. It should shut them up when they know the company is doing everything it can to control the situation."

" So who do I see out there?"

"Edward Thompson, the personnel manager. He and the president are the only ones who will know you're in the plant."

"How long have I got?"

"As long as it takes. Give me your ID card."

Foley removed the card from his wallet, tossed it on the desk and started for the door.

"By the way," Hudson asked quietly, "did Mr. Casey say anything about the accident?"

Foley removed his hand from the doorknob. "What accident?"

"He must have forgotten to mention it. The last man we sent out was killed in an industrial accident a few weeks ago."

"Casey has a convenient memory," said Foley, shaking his head and walking back to the desk. "Tell me about it."

"It was a new man, his first assignment so you wouldn't have known him. He was helping stack heavy cartons and some of them toppled over on him."

"What did the agency do about it?"

Hudson extended his hands, palms upward, in a gesture of helplessness. "There wasn't anything we could do. There was no reason to doubt it was an accident and if we had made a fuss it would have blown our cover."

Foley stalked to the door, flung it open, said, "The agency's about as concerned over one of its men getting killed as Kirklin is about employees losing their paycheck," and slammed it behind him.

Angry dark clouds seemed to suddenly boil up from the lake, sending small craft scurrying for the protection of harbors from Sandusky to Ashtabula as Foley drove east toward the Kirklin Truck Company factory. He was a harbinger of the approaching storm as he wheeled into a parking space, slammed the door of his

70

battered Ford sedan and strode toward a white sign reading Personnel Office.

He was ushered directly into Thompson's office, the icy glares of those waiting for interviews accompanying him to the door. After a few moments of conversation he was handed an application. He completed it quickly, filling most of the spaces with factual information. Age: 31; Height: 5-10; Weight: 165; Hair: black; Eyes: gray; Complexion: ruddy; Scars: three inch vertical, left cheek. The eight years he had worked for Wellington's were covered by a few fictitious jobs.

Thompson made a phone call, stood up and said, "Bob Briggs, the foreman you'll be working for, will be right down. He'll do the actual hiring, but since I called him personally there'll be no problem." He took Foley to a table in the outer room and returned to his office.

A few minutes later Briggs came in. He was all business, a man Foley would have pegged as a factory foreman if they had met on the outside. Briggs studied the application a few minutes, asked several questions and said, "O.K., I'll hire you. You start at seven Monday morning. Here's a pass, come to the main gate and ask for Department C-3."

It was an hour drive for the Kirklin plant in Cleveland to the small house Foley owned in Akron, but he detoured to catch the last few races at Thistledown. Hell, he thought as he walked to the rail, if I'm going to bet on the nags it won't hurt to know the names of a few of them.

Sunday evening he drove to his father's house in East Akron, the house where he had spent his boyhood in the shadow of the Goodyear plant.

"Pop," he said, "I'm going on secret for awhile so be careful what you say if anybody asks about me. Remember, you never heard of Wellington's."

Patrick Foley's face contorted in disgust. "That's so stupid," he said. "Hell, everybody's heard of Wellington's, and it'd be nice once in awhile to be able to tell somebody what your son does for a livin' besides bein' a drifter who hangs out in Cleveland all the time. Everybody thinks you're either a bum or a gangster. Anyway, I thought you didn't work under cover anymore. What's goin' on?"

"A special job at Kirklin Truck Company. You know, the place where they make the Kirklin *Wildcat.* "

"I oughtta know. Practically get run off the road by 'em every time I go out."

Foley laughed a little. "Come on, Pop, it's not that bad."

"Well, I don't like 'em and I don't like the idea of you goin' under cover again."

"It's no big deal, just part of the job."

The older man shook his head. "Better be careful, Ferg. I spent enough years in the rubber shops to know what the men think of a stoolie."

The word irritated Foley. "Damn it, Pop," he said, "I'm not nuts about it myself. I don't like reporting on guys I work with, but it's agency policy, so as long as I work for the people I'll do it their way."

"I suppose you'll be carryin' tales about what the union's doin' back to the bosses."

"You know better than that, Pop. I've told you a dozen times there's a federal law against reporting union activities. Besides, a lot of the things we do helps the workers."

"Like what?"

"Like . . . like, well, like reporting fire extinguishers that are overdue for recharging or if they don't keep enough toilet paper in the rest-rooms. And that one place I worked right after I started with the agency, remember? They piped music into the warehouse to make it more pleasant?"

His father snorted. "Big deal. How d'ya suppose the men ever get by before you guys come along? Let me tell you, son, you'd better not let 'em catch on to what you're doin' or you'll be in serious trouble."

"I know that, Pop," Foley said, standing up, tousling the older man's gray, wiry hair and walking to the door. "Quit worrying, I'm not exactly a greenhorn and besides, I need the extra dough. I'll keep everything I make at the plant and get half my agency pay to boot. I also keep anything I win on horse bets but get reimbursed for losses."

"Lotta good that'll do you," Patrick Foley shouted at the closing door, "if you spend the next six months in the hospital!"

Foley drove the shortest route to the Kirklin factory Monday, one that took him through a neighborhood that could be dangerous even at six-thirty in the morning. He bought a scratch sheet at a cigar store near the plant, checked in and was waiting for Briggs at seven o'clock.

"Come along," Briggs said. "I'll introduce you to Eddie King and he'll show you what to do."

King was black, friendly, capable. It took him less than half an hour to show Foley everything there was to know about the job of keeping one section of the single assembly line in the building supplied with parts.

"I'll be around if you have any questions," King said and left Foley on his own.

The huge old building was dark and dreary despite banks of fluorescent tubes and skylights along the length of the roof. Two large cranes ran on rails high above both legs of the assembly line that began at the north end of the building, looped at the south and returned so the completed cab-behind-engine *Wildcat* tractors left the line only thirty yards from the starting point. Foley cast a wary eye at the cranes and made a mental note to stay out from under them.

The clatter of machinery was the only noise for the first hour but then, for a reason Foley couldn't comprehend, men began talking to their neighbors along the line. Some drifted to other stations where they spoke to another briefly before returning to their jobs.

"What's going on?" Foley asked Eddie King when he saw him.

"Bad news for you, I'm afraid. They just spread the word that five hundred people are gonna be laid off in a month so you'll be one of 'em."

"That's what everybody's talking about?"

King shook his head. "Naw, they're bumping guys off their jobs. It goes by seniority so there'll be a lot of shuffling around until those that'll stay line up the best job they can find."

Foley watched the activity with mixed feelings of amusement and pity for those involved. Shortly before the eleven o'clock lunch break a man walked up to him, grinned and said, "I'm bumpin' you."

Shrugging his shoulders, Foley asked, "How long've you worked here?"

"Little over five years."

Foley shook his head. It was a sad business, but the only thing it meant to him was that he'd be working under a deadline. He had four weeks — nineteen more working days — to complete the assignment or forget it.

When the lunch whistle sounded Foley took his brown bag and sat down near a dozen other men, unfolded the scratch sheet and began looking it over. The others, interested only in discussing the layoff, paid no attention to either him or the sheet.

His skimpy meal finished, Foley walked along the shut down line, saw Eddie King and said, "I read where a guy was killed here a few weeks back. Was it in this building?"

"Right down there," King said, jerking his head toward the area south of the loop in the line. "Over there on the other side where those big cartons are stacked. Three rows of 'em fell over and he was in the way."

The next time his common laborer duties took him near the boxes Foley slipped behind the high stacks and examined them. Each carton was a foot high, three feet along each side and weighed about a hundred pounds. They were carefully arranged twenty to a pile. Pushing even one stack over would be impossible for a lone man. Still, he thought to himself, it had been accomplished. The solid stacks hadn't toppled without help and he was convinced his predecessor's death had been no accident.

Foley learned two other things his first week at Kirklin: Pulling out a scratch sheet at lunchtime was fruitless; and if Casey's estimate of the weekly haul Digger Brown was making in the plant was anywhere near target it was a remarkably well-concealed operation. Making a contact that would lead him to one of the books wasn't going to be easy.

The reports he wrote at home each evening and mailed to Arnold Gatewood, a non-existent person, at a post office box were routine and dull. If Casey, Hudson or Bob Hartley, the other assistant manager, were depending on the reports signed "No. 34" for interesting reading they had been disappointed for five days running.

The first three days of the second week proved just as frustrating so Foley, growing more impatient daily, made his first overture when he found himself along in a stockroom with Eddie King. "Know anywhere around here where I can place a bet on the ponies?" he asked.

King, looking at him with disgust, said, "I thought you were too smart to throw your money away like that."

Foley grinned. "I don't spend much on it. It's just a hobby with me."

"Well, I can't help you. A couple of guys in the paint shop handle numbers, but I don't know any bookies in the plant." King laughed, punched Foley's arm and added, "I make it a point not to and if you're smart you'll do the same."

The following noon the first interest was shown in Foley's scratch sheet. "Can I see that a second?" asked a man he'd seen working near the far end of the line.

"Sure," Foley replied, handing it to him. The man studied it a moment and returned it without comment.

"Where can I make a bet around here?" Foley asked.

The man stared at him a few seconds, shrugged and said, "Beats me."

At the beginning of the third week he expanded his territory, wandering into areas of the plant where he had no business to be and spending his lunch breaks sneaking into some of the dozen other buildings inside the brick wall. He saw assembly lines where two different model tractors were put together and departments where a variety of other tasks were performed. Of gambling he saw nothing.

As he'd done at the end of the first and second weeks, Foley spent Saturday morning lounging in the tavern owned by Mike Kravich, drinking beer and reading the *Daily Racing Form*. He hadn't seen Kravich in the plant and saw him only once in the tavern.

Spending Saturday afternoons at the track hoping to see a familiar face also proved a waste of time. He'd try to sneak the beer money along with what he spent at Thistledown through on his expense sheet, he decided, but the three days of his own time were a donation to the cause. Risky or not, he'd have to shake the bushes more vigorously the final week if he was going to avoid the embarrassment of reporting back to the office Friday afternoon empty handed.

He bought a scratch sheet as usual Monday morning but rather than keeping it concealed except at lunch time he folded it so that it protruded several inches above his shirt pocket and could easily be read by anyone.

"Better not let Bob Briggs see you with that," cautioned Eddie King.

Foley smiled, said, "What's he going to do, fire me?" and went on his way.

Several men gave the sheet a double take without commenting. At mid-morning Briggs saw it, looked penetratingly at Foley but said nothing. For the first time Foley wondered if Briggs suspected he was a plant. If so, had he passed his suspicion along? Foley doubted that Briggs was involved, but knew he'd been fooled before.

Shortly before lunch he was unloading boxes of Kirklin *Wildcat* nameplates at the line when the man who attached them to the tractors said, "Hey, lemme take a look at that," and pulled the scratch sheet from Foley's pocket. "I was late this morning, didn't have time to get one," the man murmured while checking the sheet.

"Yeah!" he said, his face lighting up. "I figured *Lazy Eddie* would be runnin' today. He's due, pal, and today's the day; it'll be a heavy track."

"Gonna bet him?" Foley asked.

"Hell, yes! I've been watchin' him. He's due and look at those odds. Better put somethin' on him yourself."

"Wish I could," Foley said, long faced, "but he's running in the third, so it'll be over before quitting time."

"So what?"

"So by the time I can call it'll be too late."

The man laughed. "You mean you don't bet until you get outta here?"

"How?" Foley asked. "The only book I know's in Akron, so by the time I can call it's too late for anything but the last couple of races."

"Hell, man do it right here! You mean you don't know nobody?"

Foley shook his head.

"See that door over there?" the man said, nodding toward one at the southeast corner of the building near a scrap loading dock. "Be there a couple of minutes before one and I'll take you to somebody."

"Great!" Foley said, even more elated than he showed. "I'll really appreciate it."

He was at the door at four minutes before one, a light carton in hand so an observer would think he was doing his job. The man, walking fast, appeared on schedule, opened the door and said, "Come on, we have to hurry."

Foley followed him across a brick courtyard to another building. " What's your name ?" the man asked as they entered.

"Foley. Ferg Foley. What's yours?"

"Charlie," the man replied, continuing swiftly along a narrow corridor, turning left and then entering a restroom.

A tall, muscular, black-haired man wearing horn-rimmed glasses was standing by the two basins in the small room. He looked Foley over without changing expression, turned to Charlie and said, "Who's this?"

"Foley," Charlie answered, "He's okay. He works with me and wants to put somethin' on *Lazy Eddie* like I told him to." While he talked, Charlie took a twenty from his wallet, handed it to the man and said, "On his nose in the third."

Foley removed a ten and a five from his own wallet. "This on *Lazy Eddie* to win in the third," he said, handing over the ten, "and five on *Mollie 's Delight* in the fifth."

"Foley, is it?" the man said, writing in a small notebook.

"Right," Foley replied and hurried after Charlie, who was already out the door. Two men entered as he left.

"That didn't take long," Foley said when he overtook Charlie. "What's that guy's name?"

"Slater. He's there every day at one o'clock if you wanna go back anytime."

"Thanks, Charlie, I really appreciate it."

Mission accomplished, he thought. Now if he could just see Hudson's face when he read his report Wednesday morning. He wouldn't know whether to be happy that someone had finally gotten the job done or sad because that someone had to be Foley.

On the drive home he tuned in the station that carried the results

from Thistledown. *Lazy Eddie* and *Mollie's Delight,* he discovered had something in common. Both finished fifth.

His luck didn't improve when he sought out Slater at one o'clock on Tuesday and Wednesday and bet two horses each day. One finished third but *Lazy Eddie* could have beaten the other three.

Relaxed now, Foley thought more and more about the stacked cartons and the so-called accident. When he left the plant Wednesday afternoon he drove downtown to the library, got out the previous month's microfilm of the *Plain Dealer* and began hunting. It took him nearly an hour to find the short story buried on page thirty-two.

The victim, according to the newspaper account, had been helping a forklift operator when the stacks fell on him. It didn't make sense to Foley and looking the area over again the next day didn't clarify it for him.

There was an empty space about thirty feet square behind the stacks, which was hard for him to understand in itself. Why not, he thought, stack the cartons against the wall? Anyone walking straight past the stacks to the south would enter a stockroom door. To the north another row of boxes ran off at a right angle with a ten-foot opening between them. The arrangement created a room enclosed by brick walls on two sides and twenty-foot high rows of boxes on the other two. If there was a good reason for stacking them that way it escaped Foley. He was tempted to forget the betting on Thursday. Why press his luck? Three contacts, six bets, were enough. It was money that lured him back to the restroom, the possibility of scoring on a couple of long-shots and picking up a nice bonus to offset the three day's work without pay.

The restroom was deserted when he arrived. He waited until five after one but no one came in. He watched as the seconds grew into minutes and the uneasiness building within him kept pace. When he left, the corridors seemed darker and the open courtyard he had to cross seemed wider than before.

After making two quick deliveries to the line he sought out Charlie. "Hey," he said, "I went over at one o'clock but Slater wasn't there."

Charlie's grin was taunting. "There's a lawman in the plant," he said and, after pausing to stare a moment at Foley, "It isn't you, is it?"

"Me?" Foley laughed as he spoke. "Hell, no. That's a good one."

For a few seconds they sized each other up, chuckling a little as they did so, and then Foley walked away. Charlie hadn't been laughing with him.

At quitting time Foley waited until the line at the time clock dwindled before punching out. The initial rush was over before he hurried through the main gate. It wasn't the time to have other bodies pressed closely against his.

He appraised the street, saw nothing to arouse his suspicion, and walked swiftly to his car. From the beginning he had shunned the company parking lot in favor of a spot on the main street. There are times, he had discovered long before, when it's nice to have people around. And, too, tampering with a car is more difficult on a busy street than in a deserted parking lot.

He reached the car without incident and found it apparently undisturbed. There were no fresh marks in the accumulation of dust and dirt on the hood and front fenders. The tip of the paper match was where it should be, barely visible at the rear edge of the hood on the passenger's side. The full book of matches on the driver's seat was lined up with the seat-cover pattern as he'd left it. Most important of all, a long hair still hung inconspicuously from the low side of the steering wheel.

The checks were the same he had used since shortly after going to work for the agency. They weren't foolproof, not if bomb experts from Youngstown handled a job, but they were reassuring, better than nothing certainly.

His eyes were on the rear-view mirror more than the street ahead until he was well away from the plant. He followed a different route than usual and when he felt certain no one was following he lit a cigarette, relaxed and thought ahead to his last day at Kirklin. He toyed with the idea of not going in at all and thought about calling Casey for instructions. But if he stayed away, he decided, it would remove all doubt from the minds of those involved, if any still existed, that he was a spy.

Friday morning passed slowly but uneventfully. As one o'clock approached Foley considered going back to the restroom, playing dumb. If he did, he decided, he wouldn't be playing, it would be the real thing.

The stacks of heavy cartons still intrigued him. How had they been toppled? It dawned on him when a giant, oversized forklift passed with a bulky load. He had been thinking of standard forklifts, had forgotten they also had monstrous ones in the plant. With one of them all it would take would be a ram of some sort rigged on the forks or perhaps nothing more than wedges under the rear of several cartons halfway up the stack and then a solid blow. But how could something like that be proved weeks after the fact?

He was pouring bolts from a cardboard box into a bin half an hour before quitting time when instinct warned him he was being watched. He looked up to find three men standing shoulder-to-shoulder fifteen feet away. Mike Kravich, Slater and a hard character he hadn't seen before. He was cut off from the working area, boxed into the deserted south end of the building.

Foley continued pouring bolts into the bin, appearing casual, unconcerned. He weighed his options. The smart thing, the safest, would be to disregard the rules, suddenly dash across the moving assembly line and run north to where dozens of men were working. An overt move by the trio was unlikely. Witnesses weren't included in their plans.

He knew they were counting on him to follow the usual routine, pick up the empty boxes and carry them to the scrap area. That would mean walking past the stack of cartons. They didn't realize he was on guard, didn't know the element of surprise would be on his side rather than theirs.

He shook the last of the bolts from the box, reached down and picked up the other empty ones and began walking toward the stacks. Three rows near the center were tilted slightly outward. It was set up for him and the sudden roar of a motor from the other side of the cartons confirmed it.

He continued walking unhurriedly, didn't look behind but could hear them following. Just before reaching the tilted stacks he tossed the boxes aside, sprinted ahead and made a desperate leap for the stockroom door as the cartons began crashing down. It was closer than he expected. One more row toppling would have crushed him under the tangled pile of torn boxboard and heavy parts.

A wave of animal-like fury pushed aside the fear that had momentarily come over him. His eyes darted around in search of some sort of weapon but found none so he pulled a small ring knife for cutting twine from his pocket and slipped it on the middle finger of his left hand. Quickly he hoisted himself up on the carton on the near side of the rent in the stacks.

The driver was still on the seat of the giant forklift, unaware his intended victim had escaped. Foley hurled himself at the man, bringing his left fist downward in a sweeping motion so the ring knife slashed the flesh from his ear to his jaw. His cry of agony was cut off as Foley flung him from the seat to the concrete floor.

Foley slid into the seat, threw the forklift into reverse, swung to the left and-then lurched forward so the wheels rolled over the man's legs. From the corners of his eyes he saw Slater coming through the breach so he turned sharply to the right. The right fork, waist high, caught Slater on the knee while he was still in the air. The snapping sound was audible above the roar of the motor and Slater plunged forward, crushing his glasses and his face on the fork.

Foley threw the lift into reverse again as the man he didn't know came through the opening at the left and jumped to the floor. The lift sped toward him, Foley intent on impaling him on the left fork. A terrified shriek formed on his lips but was quickly squelched as he slid between the forks an instant before the machine struck the full length of his body, sending him crashing into the cartons and then slumping to the concrete.

Now only Kravich was left. Foley jumped from the lift to the low cartons, saw him standing only a few feet away, shock masking his face. Foley leaped again, smashing into Kravich shoulder high, landing on top of him as they hit the floor. The ring knife dug into Kravich's cheek as Foley's hands went for his throat, compressing like the jaws of a vice until Kravich's eyes bulged and his face turned purple.

It was Eddie King who tore Foley's fingers loose, jarred him from his murderous rage. He needed a few seconds to grasp what had taken place before he said, "Get the plant police, Eddie, and tell them to call the city. Fast."

Bob Briggs and several others ran up as King departed. "What the hell happened?" Briggs shouted.

Foley, his composure returning but still short of breath, inhaled deeply and said, "We've got four guys here who tried to commit murder, and I think we're going to find they were successful at it a couple of months ago."

Briggs climbed on the cartons, looked over, turned back, his face ashen, and said, "My God!" He motioned to a man nearby. "Have the plant police call an ambulance." He glanced back over his shoulder and said, "Better make it two."

It was two minutes to five when Foley walked into the agency, turned left and headed down the hallway toward Casey's office. He paused in front of an open door when he saw Hudson, ready to quit for the weekend, shrugging his arms into a suit coat.

"You know those people Kirklin's going to fire?" Foley said.

Hudson, eyes widening as he took in Foley's disheveled appearance, nodded his head.

"Well," Foley continued, "Thompson or somebody's going to have to go to the hospital and the jail to break the news to four of them. Three are flat on their backs and another — Kravich — is behind bars."

"What hap — " Hudson said but Foley was gone. Hudson followed him into Casey's office as the manager looked up from the magazine he was reading and said, "Ferg. you're late. I expected you by three-thirty."

Foley sneered at him, snorted through his nose and flopped down in a chair. "Casey," he said, "if you can tear yourself away from that magazine you might be interested to know one of your investigators was murdered out at Kirklin a while back. Captain Locascio at the city is working on it, and I think he's going to be able to hang it on some people out there. I know he can get them for assault with intent to kill."

He let them absorb it for a moment and then told the story. Hudson was shocked by the violent climax but Casey took it in stride.

"Well," he said, "I'm glad you made it all right. Now that you're out of the plant I don't think there's anything to worry about but it might be better if you stay out of that neighborhood for awhile."

"I don't think Digger Brown's boys are going to care what neighborhood I'm in."

"Don't be silly, Ferg," Casey said. "It was an internal problem at the plant. Brown's too smart to get involved in it."

"I hope you're right," Foley replied, "but I'm not betting on it."

"Speaking of betting, how did you do on the ponies?"

"I dropped forty-five bucks. It'll be on my expense voucher."

Casey chuckled. "That was a chance few people ever get and you blew it."

Foley stood up and walked to the door. "I want a hot shower, clean clothes, a drink and a thick steak in that order," he said. "I hope Digger Brown doesn't have other things in mind for me."

He had closed the door behind him when Casey called, "Hey, Ferg!"

Foley poked his head back in, glowered when he saw the manager's smart-alecky grin and slammed the door shut as Casey said, "I forgot to tell you, Ferg, have a nice weekend."

Another tongue-in-cheek filler from Mike Shayne Mystery Magazine.

WATER IN A TEACUP

The old lady closed the door behind her and looked hesitatingly around the small restaurant. The jacket she wore had been fashionable in its day. Now it was frayed and tattered, like the loose-fitting dress that countless washings had faded to an unrecognizable hue. The hat that fit snugly over her gray hair dated back to the Flapper Era.

It was mid afternoon so few of the tables were occupied. After a few seconds the old lady, who weighed no more than ninety pounds and stood only five feet even in thick-heeled shoes that had seen hard use, moved as quickly as she was able to a small table for two close to the wall. She carefully set a brown paper shopping bag next to a chair and sat down.

Three waitresses were on duty. Two of them immediately sized her up as a small tipper and busied themselves elsewhere. The third, Millie Thomason, was aware of what they were doing. She gave a little shrug and walked to the old lady's table. As she took a pencil and pad from an apron pocket she smiled automatically. After all, a smile didn't cost anything.

The old lady smiled back. "Just a cup of hot water, dearie." Her voice, like the rest of her, was brittle with age.

"Nothing else?"

The old lady shook her head. Again Millie shrugged imperceptibly and walked away. When she returned with the cup of water and a spoon, she waited half expectantly. When it became apparent that her duties had been fulfilled, Millie went back to her station and, turning, looked toward the table where the old lady was seated.

She had taken a folded paper napkin from a pocket of her jacket. She turned back the corners, revealing a tea bag that had already seen service on one or more occasions. The old lady picked it up and carefully placed it in the cup of hot water, jiggling it vigorously and then pressing the spoon against its side to squeeze out the last drop of goodness.

When it was obvious that nothing more would be forthcoming, the old lady removed the tea bag from the cup, placed it on the edge of the saucer and poured sugar from a glass container into the brew. She looked around the table hopefully but sighed when she saw there wasn't a pitcher of milk.

Millie Thomason smiled to herself. One of the other waitresses approached her, frowning. "Did you see what that old woman did?" she asked Millie. "Can you beat that for nerve?"

"So where's the harm?"

"Are you kidding? Fat lot of money we'd make with customers like her. If Mr. Subichan had seen it, he'd toss her out on her ear."

"Well he didn't see it."

The second waitress glared and walked away. Millie returned to watching the old lady. When her cup was empty she stood up, retrieved her shopping bag from beside the chair, smiled at Millie and departed. Millie cleared the table. The old lady hadn't left a tip.

She returned again the next afternoon. The routine was the same, but this time Millie brought a small container of milk with the hot water. The old lady smiled gratefully. "Thank you, dearie."

In the days that followed the old lady continued to appear promptly at three o'clock. When time allowed, Millie would sit down and chat for a minute or two and the old lady seemed to enjoy that even more than her tea. The other patrons, and their number seemed to be increasing as time went on, watched attentively, feeling the afternoon interlude was both amusing and heart warming. The feeling was not shared by the two waitresses who worked with Millie.

"What do you talk to her about?" asked the one who first had voiced an objection to the old lady's presence.

Millie smiled and said, "Oh, things."

The other waitress shook her head agitatedly. "When Mr. Subichan finds out, you'll both be sorry."

But Mr. Subichan already knew. A shrewd businessman despite his limited knowledge of the English language, he had noticed a steady increase in the daily receipts over the past weeks. A look at the waitresses order blanks, which he carefully filed away, revealed that a mid afternoon flurry of business was responsible. Curious as to why a usually quiet period of the day suddenly had become lucrative, Mr. Subichan inquired of a cook and was told the story. He correctly deduced that people were coming to see the old lady who brought her own tea bag.

Millie's co-workers grinned knowingly at each other the day Mr. Subichan departed from his habit of going home to rest during the afternoon lull. But they were disappointed. Rather than hitting the roof as they expected when the daily ritual took place, he looked on approvingly. A little milk and sugar was a small price to pay for the increased profits from those who came to watch.

And so things went on as before. But the old lady, frail from the beginning, seemed to grow steadily less sturdy and more sickly. Still she continued to come, obviously more because of Millie's companionship than the tea, which often remained untouched until Millie would gently prod her into drinking it, saying she needed the nourishment.

"But nothing tastes good lately," the old lady would complain. "Even the tea seems bitter."

Millie would pat her hand and say, "Add a little more sugar."

No one, least of all the doctor, was surprised when the old lady collapsed one day on the sidewalk in front of a free clinic two blocks from the restaurant. She was carried inside, examined briefly by the doctor who had been seeing her almost daily for a month, and pronounced dead.

While her death came as no shock to the doctor, he was stunned when, for no particular reason, a nurse began poking around in the old lady's shopping bag and soon was pulling out wads of crumpled ten and twenty dollar bills. The police were called and by the time they arrived the pile of money, which by then included fifties and hundreds, totaled more than $40,000.

A death certificate was duly signed by the doctor and the body taken away by an undertaker whose original reluctance to make a pickup at the free clinic vanished quickly when he was told of the contents of the shopping bag.

The police immediately sealed off the old lady's untidy room in a shabby hotel nearby. After a night of steady work by four officers who sorted through stacks of old newspapers page-by-page as well as searching countless other potential hiding places, it was announced that an additional $50,000 in cash had been discovered along with stocks and bonds valued at several hundred thousand.

The story was on the front page of the morning paper. At nine o'clock a lawyer appeared at police headquarters, told those in charge a number of things about the old lady and then produced a will dated only a month earlier. The story in the afternoon paper contained even more human interest than the first; the old lady had left everything to a waitress named Millie Thomason, the one person who had befriended her.

Mr. Subichan watched nervously as a horde of reporters, photographers and television crews descended on the restaurant. Until the first arrived neither he nor Millie knew the old lady had died.

His initial resentment that only Millie was named in the will was forgotten by Mr. Subichan as he posed with her for countless photographs and gave out statement after statement assuring everyone that the only reward he either wanted or expected was the satisfaction of having helped make an old lady's final weeks a little happier. Eventually he came to believe it himself.

The other waitresses, however, made no attempt to conceal their anger. A policy of sharing tips had been established long ago and did this not in a sense qualify as a tip? Millie, when confronted with the idea between interviews, smiled and shook her head. No, she told them without hesitation, it did not.

After two hours of steady questioning, posing for photographs and looking into the eyes of television cameras, Millie excused herself and walked to the employees' restroom, locking the door behind her. She opened her purse and as she did so, the smile that soon would appear in newspapers and on TV screens across the country beamed back at her from the mirror.

After all, thought Millie, she had been kind to the old lady. Certainly no one else had. She reached in the purse, pushing aside a travel folder extolling the virtues of life on the Cote d'Azur, and extracted a small vial containing a powdery white substance. It had done its job well, even more effectively and quickly than Millie had hoped. Still smiling, she gave it a final look of gratitude before flushing it away forever.

MAMA'S DARLING

Mama calls me her darling. It's kind of babyish since I'm eight-years-old, but I like it. She called me that last night because I was late for supper and she was worried. She might not have called me her darling if she knew I was down in the marsh.

Mama doesn't let me go down in the marsh. She says it's a bad place and a little girl could get hurt. That's stupid because I go there all the time ever since the day last summer when I followed Billy Johnson and Tommy Syphert. I saw them going down the path between our house and Mrs. Edgecomb's. That's where the marsh really starts only it's just a little stream that comes from a pipe under the street.

I don't like Billy Johnson because he made a face at me and said girls aren't allowed down in the marsh. He and Tommy Syphert tried to chase me but I followed them anyway.

Billy Johnson was on our street all day today when the police cars were here looking for Mrs. Edgecomb's husband. Billy was nice today because I know Mrs. Edgecomb and told him about her and her husband and he thought it was funny because Mrs. Edgecomb lost her cat last week and her husband yesterday. We laughed and he gave me a bite of his candy bar so I guess I like him better than I did the day I followed him down to the marsh.

He didn't even know I was following him and neither did Tommy Syphert until after they passed the first big tree where the path ends and you come to the tall grass. You have to turn left and the path is there again but not as wide as before. Then you follow it to another big tree and the path ends for good.

That's where Billy Johnson saw me and started acting stupid. He said girls can't go to the marsh because they don't know how to do things like that and would sink in the quicksand.

"It's right over there," he said, "and you are so dumb you would walk right in it if I hadn't told you because it looks like the path goes right there but there isn't a path any more so it fools you."

I didn't believe him because everybody knows Billy Johnson is a liar. Even the teacher because she caught him. I watched him and he went to the big tree and so did Tommy Syphert. They turned real close to it and went that way.

When they were gone I went to the big tree and looked at where Billy Johnson said it was quicksand. It didn't look any different to me so I found a rock and threw it there and it sank. I found a bigger rock and threw it there and it sank too so I thought maybe it was quicksand.

Then I followed Billy Johnson and Tommy Syphert again. If you looked real close you could see where they walked because it's kind of wet and makes footprints.

After you go a long way you come to a lake with trees growing in it. I went back then because there was a big snake like mama is afraid of. The kind that opens its mouth real wide and is all white and ugly inside. I threw a rock at it because mama said its name is a cottonmouth snake. But mama yells even when she sees a little garter snake and says it is a cottonmouth snake.

When I went back I threw another rock and it sank too. I wanted something bigger but there wasn't anything except a big stick. I threw it and it just laid there so I thought maybe it really wasn't quicksand and Billy Johnson was telling another lie.

All the times I went down in the marsh I took something to throw there. Sometimes they sank and sometimes they just laid there like the stick but the next time I would go they were gone. But that didn't prove it was quicksand until last week.

Mama doesn't like Mrs. Edgecomb's cat named Iva because she says it eats birds. I never saw it eat a bird but I don't like Iva because she raises her back and makes a funny sound when you walk by her.

Last week when I went down to the marsh Mrs. Edgecomb's cat Iva was on the path trying to eat a bird. I made a noise and the bird flew away. Iva turned her head and looked at me but she didn't run like she usually does. I grabbed Iva and held her way out because she was kicking her legs and making a funny sound. I had a rubber ball to throw where Billy Johnson said it was quicksand, but I dropped it and threw Iva.

It was funny. She couldn't get her legs out and she kept moving around and making a real funny sound and all the time she kept getting lower and lower. Pretty soon just her head was there and she quit making the funny sound and looked at me and then she was gone. I guess Billy Johnson wasn't telling a lie this time.

Mrs. Edgecomb and her husband Mr. Edgecomb looked all over for Iva but they couldn't find her. It was funny because I knew where she was. I couldn't tell because mama would be mad if she knew I was down in the marsh.

I don't like Mrs. Edgecomb's husband because he is mean and always is working in his yard. He gets mad if you step on his grass and he yelled and chased me the day my ball rolled in his yard. He is just like Mr. Kincaid who lives across the street and is always working in his yard and gets mad if you go on it. I go on it when he isn't looking.

Yesterday I was going down to Mary Ellen's house and Mr. Edgecomb was mowing his lawn so I asked him if he found his cat Iva and laughed. He stopped mowing his lawn and his face was red so he got a big handkerchief out of his pocket and wiped it. He kept looking at me but didn't say anything so I said, "I know where your cat is right now but I won't tell you."

He said some things and I said some things and then he said, "I will give you a piece of candy if you tell me where Iva is," so I said, "Come with me and I will show you where Iva is."

Mr. Edgecomb followed me to where the big trees are so mama can't see me go down to the marsh. He followed me along the stream to the first big tree and we turned left and were walking to the next big tree when he got mad and said, "I will beat the hell out of you if you are leading me on a goose chase."

I don't know what a goose chase is but he was mad so I stuck my tongue out at him and put my thumbs in my ears and waved my fingers at him like Billy Johnson does. He started to chase me so I ran to the big tree and jumped behind it just before he caught me. But Mr. Edgecomb didn't turn left like you are supposed to but went straight ahead and right away was up to his knees.

It was funny because he waved his arms around and said, "My God," and pretty soon he was almost up to his belt.

I was laughing but he said, "My God, please help me," but how could I help him? Besides he was up over his belt by then and he kept saying, "My God," and, "Please go get somebody," and, "Please run fast."

I didn't want to go because he would have been clear gone by the time I got back. And besides, then mama would have found out I was down in the marsh.

Mr. Edgecomb put his arms out flat but they went too and when it got up to his neck he put his head back and didn't ask me to go any more. He kept saying, "Oh, my God," over and over until it went in his mouth and then he kind of looked back at me over the top of his head with his eyes and then they were gone too.

I went on down by the lake with the trees in it. The cottonmouth snake was there again but he squiggled away like he was afraid of me. On the way back I found a big rock and threw it and wondered if it went on top of Mr. Edgecomb's head.

That's why I was late for supper and mama was worried. She put her arms around me and said, "Thank God. Where has Mama's Darling been?"

All day the police cars have been on our street looking for Mrs. Edgecomb's husband. Once I saw Mrs. Edgecomb out in her yard talking to them and twisting her handkerchief around and crying. I thought about telling but I couldn't because then mama would have found out I was down in the marsh. I would have been in trouble and she wouldn't have made the popcorn and brought it out on the porch so we could sit on the swing and eat it.

She said, "Why is Mama's Darling so quiet?" but I didn't answer her because I was watching Mr. Kincaid mow his lawn across the street. I wonder if he ever goes down in the marsh?

MYSTERY MINIQUIZ

In the early forties, actress Glenda Farrell starred as a wise-cracking reporter, with Barton MacLane as her policeman associate, in a series of cinematic second features. What was the name of the character she portrayed in these films?

Torchy Blane.

Who murdered Mary Anne Nicholls and Marie Kelly?

They were the first and last prostitutes murdered by Jack the Ripper.

What British school did James Bond attend?

007 went to Eton.

What happened at Bodego Bay?

The Birds attacked the residents in the 1963 Hitchcock movie.

In the late 1930's Twentieth Century Fox produced a series of mysteries starring Peter Lorre in the lead role. What was the name of the sleuth in these movies?

Lorre played the Japanese detective Mr. Moto.

What do Warner Oland, Sidney Toler, and Roland Winters have in common?

They all portrayed Charlie Chan on the screen.

A Mike Shayne Mystery Magazine quiz.

THE HABITUALS

It'll be the first time I've worked in better than three years so I'm a little excited about it as I turn off the interstate and head east on Route 28.

It looks like a nice set-up. I'll be working with a couple of old friends: Ernie Strickland on the seat beside me and Roger McNarney, waiting for us in Midland. The fourth will be a guy named Tom Bridges. I've never met him but he's handled the preliminaries.

"We'll go right by the store in a few minutes so you can take a look if you want to." The speaker is Joan Hulbert, Ernie's older sister. She's in the back seat along with Bridges' wife, Amy. Mrs. Bridges picked us up in Fort Wayne and it's her car I'm driving.

I think about it a minute and say, "Okay, we'll look, but just from the outside."

Ernie stirs, chuckles a little and says, "Yeah, good idea. I don't like to shop on Friday afternoon. Too crowded."

It's the first time he's opened his mouth since we started out an hour ago. I give him a halfway smile, poke his arm and say, "When in hell did you ever do any grocery shopping?"

He draws himself up in the seat and fakes a hurt look. "Lots a times," he tells me. "I'm very domesticated."

That deserves a horse laugh and he gets it. I like Ernie, he's a good man to work with, but he worries me a little because he's so damned unpredictable. Not on a job — he's all business then — but other times when he's relaxed, enjoying himself.

Ernie's one of those guys who fools a lot of people. His exuberance, the outward signs of friendliness and joviality, misleads them. Anyone who really knows him realizes that the time to be wary of Ernie is when he's happy. I don't know why it is but when he's having fun, has had a few drinks, it only takes a word or a facial expression to make something snap inside him. When that happens it pays to be cautious even if you're his friend.

Amy leans forward and says, "That's it up ahead on the right."

I turn into the parking lot and stop near the highway a good seventy-five yards from the big, one-story building faced with dark brown brick. There are eight automatic glass doors and in front of them a covered drive-up area. About a hundred cars are parked around it.

Ernie chuckles again and slaps his leg. "Perfect," he says. "Not a window in the place. Made to order, hey buddy?"

I nod. He's right except I'm not crazy about the traffic pattern. There are two entrances to the parking lot off the highway and another from a side street. The side street leads to an expensive residential area and Amy says that from it you can get to a couple of other additions or go south to the college a mile away.

"How far are we from town?" I ask.

"About three miles from downtown on the highway," Amy replies. "It's built up from here on in and there's a big shopping center a little way down the road."

"Many side streets?"

"Lots of them."

I'm not completely happy with the arrangement, but it could be worse. I pull back on the road and head toward town. It's a six minute drive to the Bridges' house so it's convenient but still not too close to the store.

Roger McNarney is waiting when we arrive. It's the first time I've seen him in nearly four years so we greet each other warmly. We used to work together a lot and respect each other's ability. Roger's quiet, soft spoken. He's about thirty-five, a good looking guy around six feet tall with well-groomed brown hair and friendly brown eyes that win people's confidence right away.

We are still reminiscing when Bridges comes in. I dislike him at first sight. He's the salesman type, too outgoing, too sure of his own charm to suit me. He comes on strong with a pearly grin and hearty manner like we all are old buddies.

His approach falls flat but he doesn't have the brains to know it. While he rattles on I keep one eye on Roger and the other on Ernie. Roger is a little amused but Ernie hunches down in his chair and his eyes narrow as Bridges croons away.

Bridges must be close to twenty-five but he's still in college. He's a big, husky guy with a bushy mustache and even white teeth that he likes to show. He takes a bottle of bourbon from a cabinet and says, "Anyone care for a drink?" .

"Put it away."

Bridges' smile fades. He stares at Ernie in surprise and says, "What?"

"I said put the goddam stuff away!"

Bridges' mouth goes slack and he says, "Oh," weakly. The bottle goes back in the cabinet and he has a stunned expression as he murmurs, "Okay." Suddenly he seems to comprehend that he isn't with his college crowd or spreading the charm at a Chamber of Commerce get-together.

He's made me apprehensive, though. He isn't the kind of man we should be working with. How in hell, I wonder, did Ernie let his sister talk him into something like this? Here we are ready to go to work and the only one who knows anything about the job is a rank amateur. I look at him and say, "Okay, lay it out for us."

Right away he's Mr. Personality again. He outlines the job like he was reciting in class and expects to get an "A" for his trouble. He doesn't do badly at that and I feel a little better. When he finishes I make a few alterations in his plan and Roger throws in a couple of changes but Ernie just sits there half smiling, eyes heavy lidded, until everyone quits talking and then he looks at Bridges and says, "Got all the stuff?"

"Right," Bridges snaps like Patton reporting to Eisenhower. "Everything's set." It wouldn't surprise me if he clicked his heels and threw a salute.

Ernie quits smiling. "Well then stop talking, fella, and get it." Bridges has just enough sense to keep his mouth shut. He's afraid of Ernie. The fear shows in his face and he's confused by it. He thought he'd be the big man, didn't realize the kind of people he was getting involved with. He's in over his head and it scares hell out of him.

Bridges goes into another room, comes back carrying a big cardboard carton and sets it on the floor in front of Ernie. Roger and I grin at each other as Ernie digs into it like some dumb, overgrown kid who's found the Christmas goodies. He tosses a couple of packages of women's nylon hose on a coffee table and then four dark blue stocking caps, the kind sailors wear. Next comes four lightweight blue wind-breakers like you see everywhere.

None of that turns Ernie on too much, but a grin spreads across his face when he pulls out an S&W .38 and then a couple of more hand guns and a sawed-off shotgun. Ernie caresses the shotgun while he says, "Why four guns?" to Bridges.

"One for each of us," Bridges answers.

Ernie leans back laughing until he's looking up at the ceiling. He stops laughing suddenly, brings his head back down and says, "None for you, college boy." Roger smiles and says, "Amen." I nod in agreement.

The three of us examine the guns and Roger and I select one. He turns to Bridges and asks, "Where'd you get these?"

"Different places. Don't worry, they can't be traced."

It's not funny but the rest of us laugh. "Yeah, I'll bet," Roger says, shaking his head. He looks at me and says, "What do you think?"

I shake my head, too, and shrug. "I don't know. I don't like it."

"Aw, what the hell," Ernie says. "We've come this far, let's go ahead." His face is expressionless as he looks at Bridges and says, "But you'd better be right about everything you've said, college boy." A tremor passes the length of Bridges' body as he stares back at Ernie's pale blue, almost transparent eyes.

We arrive at the supermarket a few minutes before it closes at eleven o'clock. Bridges is driving. Roger orders him to park at the end of the building facing the side street and to stay behind the wheel with the motor running. Ernie, Roger and I put stockings over our heads and the wool caps over them. We're wearing the blue wind-breakers and dark pants. We all have handguns but Ernie's is in his pocket and he's carrying the shotgun.

The first step goes just the way Bridges said it would. Right at eleven the assistant manager pulls his car in front of the doors, goes inside and comes back carrying a canvas bag. He's making the first run to the night depository and it's our cue to move. Before he can close the door behind him Roger sticks a gun against his head and says, "Get back out and let's go inside."

The color drains from the guy's face and his legs are rubbery when he stands up. I take the bag from him and Roger escorts him into the store with Ernie and me on each side. Ernie goes right to the checkout lines where the last customer is standing and several employees are at cash registers getting their trays ready to turn in.

To the right of the lines is an office enclosed by a five-foot barrier. I vault over it before the lone occupant, a woman, can get to the alarm which Bridges has pinpointed for us. "Do what you're told," I warn her, "or I'll blow your head off."

She just stares at me like a zombie until Roger shoves the assistant manager through the door and follows him inside. She starts blubbering then and wringing her hands. I drop a stack of blank money order forms in the bag and leave the woman and the safe to Roger.

Ernie has the people at the checkout lines shaking in their shoes and none of them makes a fuss about emptying their trays into the bag. It moves like clockwork and in less than three minutes we're running for the car. We get a shock because it's empty. We're piling in when Bridges comes out from around the side of the building where he's been hiding. For a second I think Ernie is going to let him have it, and maybe he should have.

Bridges has left the motor running. The tires screech as he throws it in gear and shoots out toward the side street right in front of a car that's using the parking lot for a short cut and has come up on us from the right rear. There is a stop street about a hundred yards from the store and the other car is right on our bumper when we reach it.

I say, "Go left," and Bridges does, starting a little smoother this time. The other car sticks with us but then turns right at the first street. Ernie, beside Bridges in front, tells him to take a right at the next intersection and then go around the block.

The other car has parked in a driveway and a kid about twenty is getting out. "Hold it," Ernie tells Bridges and when he stops at the end of the driveway Ernie starts to bring up the shotgun.

"Forget it, Ernie," I yell. "It's okay. Let's get the hell away from here and off the streets."

We get back to the house without trouble and once inside we relax, feeling pretty good. We stuff the jackets, caps and stockings in a sack to get rid of later and start counting money. Not including checks it comes to just under twenty thousand. We also have nearly a hundred blank money orders but using them will be risky. Roger says to get rid of them along with the checks. Ernie and I hate to do it, but know he's right and go along with the idea.

The women get back from someplace about then. We give each of them a thousand off the top and then split the rest four ways. A drink's in order so Ernie gets the bottle from the cabinet and pours a round. He's still burned about Bridges leaving the car like he did. Roger and I are, too, but there's nothing to do about it now so Roger says, "That's what happens when you work with an amateur. It's our fault for doing it so let's forget it."

We mellow after a couple of drinks, even Ernie, and Roger looks at Bridges, raises his glass and says, "Kid, I'll have to admit you did a pretty good job casing the place."

It puffs Bridges up again, makes him feel like a big shot. He's wearing a self-satisfied smile when he says, "Nothing to it, they were suckers. I walked in, told them I was writing a term paper on security systems and they showed me the whole layout."

It hits the rest of us like a bombshell. The smile fades after a minute of dead silence and Bridges looks at Ernie, who's gripping the arms of his chair so tight his knuckles are white, and then Roger, who just stares at him dumfounded. Lastly he looks at me and I say, "I suppose you even gave them your right name."

Bridges shakes his head and you can see the confidence start to build again. "Of course not," he says. "I'm not stupid."

"How long do you think it'll take the cops to find you?" asks Roger.

Bridges, who really is stupid, says, "How do you think they'll find me out of more than seventeen thousand students at the university?"

There's an outside chance he's right, depending on how hard the cops decide to work. There isn't much we can do about it anyway except wait and see what happens unless we take Ernie's suggestion to "kill him right now."

We spend the night at the house and leave an hour after daybreak in Roger's car. Before we start Ernie terrifies Bridges by telling him what'll happen if he's picked up and brings us into it. It won't help, though, because a couple of tough detectives will scare Bridges as much as Ernie does unless Ernie's present.

As soon as we're away from the house Ernie says, "Let's go to Naptown. There's a chippy there I wanna look up."

"Indianapolis is no place for you," Roger warns. "The cops there are already looking for you."

Ernie grins and says, "Let 'em look."

Roger shakes his head but heads for the interstate and we're in Indianapolis an hour later. Roger's living there and gives us both the number of a post office box he's rented under a phony name and a phone number where he can be reached. We drop Ernie off near Monument Circle and then drive north about fifty miles to Tipton, the little town I've decided to hole up in for a couple of weeks.

I go to a place that rents rooms by the day or week. I'm beat so I sleep a couple of hours. When I wake up I find some dirty old stationery in a desk drawer, jot down the number of the pay phone in the hallway and mail it to Roger. I buy a few paperbacks and a magazine at a newsstand and then eat supper at a hole-in-the-wall restaurant that claims to have home cooking. If the claim is true it explains the high divorce rate.

The next day's Sunday so I buy an Indianapolis Star and settle down in my room. There's a story about the robbery but not many details. The witnesses couldn't agree whether there were four or five of us. I do a lot of reading, leaving the room only to eat. Monday goes about the same way and by late afternoon I'm restless and decide to take a walk.

It's one of those rare evenings you get sometimes in late winter on the plains of Central Indiana. There's no biting wind out of the west and six or eight inches of snow on the ground. The stillness gives the quiet streets and big old houses a picture-book look. People are hurrying home after work, and there's a fresh smell to the air and a warm glow from the lights in the windows. Twilight; the hour when loneliness comes over people away from home. Even those like me who don't have a home.

The feeling doesn't linger long. I'm used to being alone. Anyone is who's spent fourteen of his thirty-three years behind bars, most of them inside the forty-foot walls at Michigan City. Still, while it lasts, the heaviness in the pit of my stomach makes me want to go back and try it again from the beginning. Try it without the craving for excitement this time.

I gave up the illusions a long time ago, those stories you tell the do-gooders until you get to believing them yourself. Bad breaks, the wrong companions, an unhappy childhood. Those are the alibis. The truth is you want to do it — crave the excitement that's part of it. I kidded myself for a couple of weeks after I left Michigan City last month. Then I ran into Ernie and couldn't wait to get back in harness when he told me about the job his sister had lined up.

Ahead of me a car pulls into a driveway and a man my age gets out, takes a briefcase from the back seat and walks to the house. A kid runs past the window to greet him at the door. For a minute I think he has something that's missing from my life, but then my fingers close on the metal object in my pocket and I know I have something that's missing from his.

I grin even though there's no one to see it, turn at the next corner and head back downtown. I'm hungry and anxious to get back to my book. I'll try a little more of that home cooking and then settle down with a bottle and the book.

A week passes and then one night the phone rings out in the hall. I hurry to it, sensing it's Roger calling.

"Can you talk?" he asks when he recognizes my voice.

"As far as I know it's okay."

"They picked up our college friend."

I've been expecting it but still it shocks me a little. "Has he said anything?" I ask.

"I'm not sure but I'm keeping in touch. I'll get back to you when I hear anything."

The next morning's Star has the story. Finding Bridges hadn't taxed the police brains too much, but we hadn't expected it would if they tried at all. It's a safe bet that he'll talk, too, so from the point of view of the rest of us Ernie had the right idea.

I'm not surprised when I look up from my supper and see Roger coming in the door. He sits down across from me and stares at the food on my plate with distaste.

"Looks like something they'd serve you up at *The City*," he says. "Of such things are prison riots made."

I laugh. Roger's dry humor always amuses me. He's smart, self-educated, always had his nose in a book when we spent seven years together at Michigan City. I did, too, but usually light stuff. Novels, things like that, or mysteries when I could get them. Roger went in more for technical reading. History and current events, too, and the classics like Shakespeare.

Funny, though, he quit school after the tenth grade the same as I did. He'd talk about it sometimes, about how most teachers can't reach certain kids, can make even the most interesting subject boring as hell. Once in awhile he'd talk about one teacher he had in ninth grade, a guy who really kindled a fire in him. Trouble was there were too many others ready to toss buckets of water until the last spark was extinguished. Roger would say he wished he could have had that one guy for every subject.

"The college boy's talked, right?" I ask.

Roger nods his head. "They've got him on armed robbery but the prosecutor's going to reduce it to theft. He'll plead guilty and get a suspended sentence and then testify against the rest of us."

"How'd you find out?"

"I've got a connection over in Midland who keeps me posted."

"Ernie was right, we should have killed him,"

"Not then," Roger says, shaking his head. "He was just dumb. Hell, anybody can be dumb, college or not. This is

105

something else. Dumb or not, you don't have to stool."

I sip my coffee and think about it. Bridges — all of us for that matter — can get ten years but in Indiana you're out in five if you keep your nose clean and earn *good time* credits. That's all Bridges has to worry about.

Not Roger, Ernie and me, though. We've all got at least two felony convictions already so they can nail us as habituals and tack on thirty more years. Even with *good time* we'd serve twenty. So the guy with the least to lose and is responsible himself for getting picked up turns around and rats on us — really has us in a bad spot.

"I talked to Ernie this afternoon," Roger says. "He's heading west for awhile. Tulsa, I guess."

Roger leans closer, shakes his head and grins. "That Ernie's really something. He just found out they're looking for him for killing somebody in a tavern parking lot over in Dayton. Ernie, or whoever it was — he claims he didn't do it — got into an argument with a guy. It wasn't much but the other guy and his friend leave so it won't go any further. Ernie — if it was him — follows them out, walks up to their car, puts a gun against the guy's head and blows his brains out."

"Sounds like Ernie," I say.

"Sure does. It really does. Stupid, just plain stupid."

We both laugh. Big, dumb old Ernie. He'd do anything in the world for you if you're his friend, but then if something got him mad he might turn around and kill you before he knew what he was doing. A big kid with a mean streak but still . . . Well, no one would understand our feeling for him.

"We'd better go someplace till things cool down," I say. "Out of state someplace."

"Right. I don't think they've got us in mind when they talk about Hoosier hospitality. Unless they mean the kind they hand out up at *The City.* "

I ride back to Indianapolis with Roger and camp on the sofa in his apartment. He finds out that Bridges pleaded guilty at his arraignment and is out on bail until he's sentenced. His wife and Ernie's sisters were arrested, too, but the charges against them have been dismissed. Warrants are out for Roger, Ernie and me. Between us Roger and I have better than seven thousand bucks so we decide to head for Florida and take it easy for awhile.

"What'll we do about Bridges?" I ask him.

"Nothing right now. We'll just sit tight and maybe none of us will get picked up before the stature of limitation runs out."

"Hell, man, that's five years!"

"I know, but you never can tell. No sense in doing anything about Bridges until we have to."

"Don't forget his wife. We've got her to worry about, too."

"No we don't." Roger says. "A good lawyer wouldn't let her testify to much since she wasn't there. The only thing that could convict any of us is Bridges' testimony."

Roger has a few loose ends to tie up before we start and I need a few things so I walk to a shopping area five blocks away and get them. I'm a block from the apartment on my way back when I see Roger being escorted to a car by a couple of cops. I duck into a doorway until they're gone.

I've got a little better than five hundred bucks in my wallet but I can kiss the three thousand in the apartment goodbye. The clothes and other stuff I had there are no big loss, but the money is.

I ride a bus downtown and get a room in a cheap hotel, buy a pair of pants, a shirt, a package of shorts and another of T shirts, three pairs of sox, toilet articles and a flight bag. I pick up a couple of more paperbacks and hole up for a few days.

The Star keeps me posted. Bridges sentence is suspended, which isn't a surprise, and Roger pleads not guilty, which isn't a surprise, either. An Indianapolis lawyer I know represents him.

I call Joan Hulbert in Fort Wayne. She tells me Ernie is in Tulsa and Amy Bridges has left her husband and is living with Joan in Fort Wayne. She's okay, Joan says, and won't testify or, if she's forced to, won't remember anything. The court agreed to the prosecutor's suggestion that Bridges be allowed to leave the state until Roger's trial comes up and he's got a public relations job with a friend in Tampa. So I'll be going to Florida after all.

I call Roger's lawyer and tell him to have Roger ask for a speedy trial. The lawyer objects at first but I convince him it's the way to go. Roger can't make bond since the money in the apartment was confiscated. The lawyer mentions money, of course, so I tell him not to worry, he knows he'll get it.

I've been watching the parking lots downtown and have picked out a car. The owner leaves it at quarter to eight every morning and doesn't come back for it until ten after five. You can set your watch by him. He works two blocks away and can't see the lot from his office. The registration is in a glassine folder on the sun visor so for a hundred a friend fixed me up with a social security card and a driver's license with the owner's name on them. It's as good a name as any.

I'm sitting on a rail with my flight bag a couple of spaces down from where he always parks when the guy arrives on the dot of seven forty-five. I'm on the interstate before eight and by the time he gets back to the parking lot I'm having supper in Chattanooga. When he goes to bed his car is at a shopping center in Atlanta and I'm in a little hotel a mile away.

I'm going to need more cash so I size up the neighborhood around the hotel. I don't like liquor store jobs – too much chance of fireworks but settle on one as the best of a poor lot. I go downtown, check the bus schedule to Savannah, leave my flight bag in a locker at the station and arrive back at the liquor store half an hour before the bus pulls out.

Everything goes smoothly. The clerk doesn't feel like playing hero so I walk out with close to four hundred dollars, jump in a cab a block away and have the driver drop me off downtown. I cover the last few blocks to the bus station on foot and get aboard five minutes ahead of schedule.

Savannah is all decked out in her spring finery and I'd like to stick around, relax awhile, spend some time walking around the little parks, but decide to push on so I catch a bus to Jacksonville the next day. From there I take one to Orlando, stay a day and then go on to Tampa.

I check into a down-at-the-heels hotel, study the classified ads and the yellow pages and then get some sleep. In the morning I go car shopping, find a nice one with New Jersey plates, and drive out to the bay area. I've got a map but it still takes nearly an hour to find the place I'm looking for.

When I leave an hour later I've rented an old hulk of a boat for a week. Up to now I've never been on anything bigger than a rowboat but figure I can handle it okay. It's got a small cabin with a bunk and some kind of chemical toilet so I'll headquarter on it.

I drive a mile or so, leave the New Jersey car at a restaurant that's got a good noontime crowd and hop a bus headed downtown. I pick out a commonplace local car, drive to a shopping center, make a quick switch of license plates – how often does anyone look at their own plates? — and should be okay for a few days of driving.

Finding Bridges turns out to be even easier than I expected. Three phone calls to public relation outfits is all it takes. When I hit the jackpot I hang up before he gets to the phone. His car, the same one and still with Indiana plates, is in a lot a block from his office. If he's trying to maintain a low profile he's not too smart about it. Maybe he's dumb enough to think it isn't necessary.

I'm waiting across the street when he leaves the office a couple of minutes after five and goes to a bar a few doors away with two other guys. He stays about an hour and then gets his car and drives a few miles to a swinging singles apartment.

I nose around and find out which apartment is his. I'm hardly back to the car before he's out again and on his way on foot to a cocktail lounge down the street. I follow him in, find a stool at the bar and look around for him. He's in a booth no more than twenty feet away with a tall blond. A couple of minutes later he looks my way but, like I figure, doesn't give me a second glance. I'm wearing dark glasses, have grown a bushy mustache and my hair's a lot longer. I finish my drink and leave.

The next morning I pick up a few supplies at a junk yard and a marine supply house. That cuts my bankroll to two hundred bucks.

In the afternoon I take the boat out. It isn't too tricky and in a few minutes I'm out in the bay. I have enough sense to make damn sure I can find my way back. I kind of enjoy it and go out quite a ways before heading in. Right after dark I go out again. I expect it to be tougher finding my way back but the lights on shore seem to make it easier.

I arrive at the cocktail lounge a little after eleven. Bridges is there again but with a brunette this time. I have a couple of drinks and go back to the boat.

I relax the next day, spend the afternoon at Al Lopez Field watching the Reds and Cardinals play a spring training game. After that I treat myself to a good steak at a place called *The Flame* and then go back to the boat and take a nap.

Bridges is in the cocktail lounge with a different blond when I arrive about ten. A little before midnight they leave and walk to his apartment. When I'm sure that's where they're headed I follow in my car and see them go inside.

In less than an hour they come out together and he walks her back to the lounge parking lot. When I drive in he's leaning in the window of her car, talking as usual. He waves when she drives away and then starts walking back to the apartment. I wait until he's almost there and then pull up alongside.

"Hi, Tom," I say heartily, friendly-like.

"Hi," he answers, grinning and walking to the car. He leans over and looks in, the grin gradually fading away. "Is it — " he says, either forgetting my name or having trouble saying it.

"Yeah, it is. Get in, I want to talk to you."

"It's late," he says, shaking his head and starting to draw back.

I pull the gun from under a handkerchief on the seat and repeat, "Get in," He starts to shake but does as he's told.

"Where are we going?" he asks as we start away.

"To a place where we can talk."

"Why not here, my place?"

"I don't like it. Too many women around."

He thinks I'm joking with him or maybe believes I'm impressed by his way with the ladies. He starts getting cocky again but that's okay with me. Puffed up or deflated, it doesn't make any difference.

"I hope you guys didn't get the idea I'd really testify against you," he says.

I chuckle a little. "Why would we think a thing like that, Tom?"

110

His confidence deserts him again when we pull up at the boat yard. He starts to stammer and doesn't want to get out of the car. I convince him it would be the smart thing to do, but have to keep the gun against the small of his back until we reach the boat.

When we get there he starts to look over his shoulder but I give him a shove and he jumps aboard. I follow and before he can think about turning around again I give him a good tap on the head with the gun butt.

I drag him inside the cabin and check his pulse. His lights are out permanently. I get his clothes off and take a look in his wallet. The seventy-three dollars will help but I wish it was more. Getting the chain around him is a job but when I'm finished the only way he'll get out is one bone at a time.

The old motor decides to be balky but I persuade it to run after a couple of minutes and before long we are well out in the bay. When I'm satisfied we're far enough from shore I cut the engine down as low as it'll go, position the two boards I brought along for the purpose against the rail, slide him out and onto them and attach a rusty old anchor to the chain. Lifting the boards is almost more than I bargained for but I finally accomplish it. I toss the boards in after him, go back to the cabin and head for shore.

I catch a few hours sleep, shave and freshen up, drive downtown, say goodbye to the car and catch an early bus north to Jacksonville. I spend the night there and then get another bus to New Orleans. By now money is tight again.

The second night there I'm sitting in a bar thinking about the best way to replenish my bankroll when I get talking to the guy on the next stool. We hit it off pretty good and it turns out he's a foreman with a tree trimming outfit and after a couple of hours he offers me a job. It's outside work and the weather's nice so I decide to take him up on it.

I call Roger's lawyer and he tells me the trial is coming up in five weeks. I tell him there's no chance Bridges will testify and to make sure there's no continuances. He says the prosecutor won't even let it go to trial without Bridges.

I also call Joan Hulbert. Amy Bridges is still living with her and has filed for divorce. I tell Joan to let her know Bridges won't contest it and isn't going to testify against

Roger. I think she gets my meaning. She tells me she and Amy won't be testifying, either.

When I quit the job a month later and catch a bus north to Memphis I have three hundred bucks in my wallet and another three hundred in a money belt. After what happened at Roger's apartment my money stays on me. I spend a couple of nights in Memphis and then take a bus to Nashville and another on in to Indianapolis.

Roger's trial has been continued two weeks because the prosecutor can't seem to locate Bridges. He wanted more time but Roger's lawyer fought against any continuance at all so the judge settled on two weeks.

I rent a halfway decent apartment close to downtown. I go out by Roger's old place and I'll be damned if his car isn't still where he left it. One tire's flat and the battery's dead but I have it running in no time.

Like any city, Indianapolis has a couple of bars where people who move in my circle can be found. I'm having a drink in one when Ernie walks in. I bust out laughing because he's grown a mustache, too. It's straw colored like his hair and droops down at both ends. He doesn't see me and I sit there laughing, watching him try to brush back both ends of it at the same time because it keeps getting in his beer.

He hears me so he turns and scowls until he realizes it's me. We celebrate old home week and bring each other up to date. I tell him: "Bridges isn't going to testify against Roger. The prosecutor can't find him and I don't think he's going to surface for awhile."

Ernie stares at me for a few seconds, puzzled like. Then the light dawns and a big grin spreads across his face. He jolts me with a punch on the arm and says, "Won't surface for awhile, huh? Hey, that's pretty good."

We talk a little more and then Ernie asks me, "You remember Ted Beckert, don't you?"

I think about it a minute and remember Beckert was at Michigan City with us for awhile about seven or eight years back. "Sure," I say, "What about him?"

"He's got something lined up over in Terre Haute. A supermarket, kind of like the last time only no amateurs. I'm in but we need a couple of more guys."

"Fine," I say. "Roger'll be out in about a week if you can wait."

It's okay with Ernie, naturally, and the next night we get together with Beckert and set things up.

I'm parked a little way up the street when Roger steps out of the jail in Midland. He looks around a few seconds and then starts walking toward downtown. I give him a little head start and then pull up beside him.

"Wanna buy a car, buddy?" I say in a stage voice. "Cheap."

He gives me a funny look, studies the car a second and then looks closer at me and grins. "Trying to peddle me a hot car, are you?" he says. "I'll have the law on you for that."

He walks around and climbs in beside me. He's got a big envelope stuffed with our money from the apartment. They had to give it back to him when they dismissed the charge.

"Where're we going?" he asks as I pull out into traffic.

"How about Terre Haute?"

"Why not?" Roger says. "A lovely city they tell me. A business trip I assume."

I nod my head and laugh. Roger always makes me laugh.

A MATTER OF ORGANIZATION

Vince Levandowski lingered on the sidewalk in front of the diner, poking halfheartedly at the remains of breakfast with a toothpick. The pale morning sunlight waged its daily battle with the haze off the lake and the smog from the factories. A light breeze from the park carried the fragrance of autumn to him. He inhaled deeply, savoring the aroma.

It was a day meant to be lazed away. The kind of day that Vince Levandowski most enjoyed because others were working and he was free. Mornings were always the best. The whole day lay before him to do with as he chose. In late afternoon when people left the shops and factories a vague discontentedness would come over him. Then, with the work behind them, the others seemed to have something he didn't have. He wasn't certain just what it was but he could feel it, knew it was there. Had anyone told him it was a sense of accomplishment he would have laughed at them.

But late afternoon was a long way off. The armed robbery charge in East Liverpool had been dismissed and Vince Levandowski was at peace with the world. Now the only problem facing him was deciding whether to walk east or west on Euclid Avenue. He flipped the toothpick toward the curb and replaced it in his mouth with a cigarette. When it was lit he tossed the match after the toothpick and struck out west at a leisurely pace.

He eyed the shop windows without enthusiasm. Then, as he was passing Rivers Jewelry Store, a large ring attracted his attention. He paused to admire it but after several seconds decided the stone was too big to be the real thing. As he started to turn away he caught sight of a figure inside the store. Grinning, he opened the door and called out, "Hey, big businessman, how you doing?"

The young man behind the counter looked up, said, "Hey, Vinnie, what you up to?" and grinned, too.

Vince stepped inside. "Nothing much. You running the place now, Bruce?"

Bruce Rivers nodded. "Pop still owns it but he doesn't come in much anymore. He made me manager."

"Well all right, buddy!" Vince aimed a friendly punch at the other's arm and then held up the thumb and forefinger of each hand as if framing a newspaper headline. "Glenwood High boy makes good."

Rivers, embarrassed a little, smiled and said, "Cut it out, Vinnie. So what are you doing, really? I've got to go downtown. Want to ride along?"

Vince considered the offer. "Sure, why not?"

As Rivers drove west on Euclid they reminisced a little, talked of former classmates awhile and then fell silent. Vince stared out the window vacantly. How, he wondered, had the armed robbery charge come to be dismissed? A phone call from Romeo Squillini the night before had given him the news but not the details. Romeo wasn't the sort of man you pumped for information. It didn't matter, though, so he forgot it, turned to Rivers and asked, "Where we headed?"

"The Garfield Building. I have to pick up a few things there." Vince chuckled. The Garfield Building was the wholesale jewelry center of Cleveland. "Maybe I will, too," he said, "if you think I can get away with it."

Rivers laughed. "Same old Vinnie. Not a chance, big fella." They parked a block from the place, an ugly stone relic on the east end of the downtown business district. Vince Levandowski was well acquainted with the Garfield Building. He often had looked it over hungrily, sometimes had pointed out that it was a plum ripe for the picking but the word from above was, "Lay off."

As they entered the lobby a harried looking, sad-eyed man of middle years stepped from the elevator. A large merchandise case was in each hand and a smaller one was tucked under one arm. His face brightened when he saw Rivers. "Bruce," he said, "How are you?" He set the cases on the floor and extended a scrawny, veined hand.

"Fine, Bernie," Rivers replied, gripping the hand. "When did you get in town?"

"Just last night, Bruce." The man was wearing a heavy overcoat that hung loosely from sloping shoulders. He wiped perspiration from his face with a handkerchief. The temperature outside was near seventy. "I was going to call you. I have some beautiful merchandise with me, really beautiful. Will you be at the store this afternoon?"

Rivers shook his head. "No, but we're open tonight. Could you stop by then? Say about seven-thirty?"

"Of course, Bruce, of course. Always at your convenience." The man stooped and retrieved his cases. He said, "At seven-thirty, then," and hurried away.

Vince Levandowski grinned. He touched the elevator button and asked, "Who was that guy?"

"Bernie Friedman, an independent salesman from New York. He carries a good line."

"Looks like a real character."

Rivers chuckled. "Yeah, I guess he is. Tries too hard to please. He's kind of shy except when he's talking about jewelry. Bernie's okay, though."

As they left the building half an hour later Vince said, "Think I'll stay downtown awhile as long as I'm here. Thanks for the lift Bruce."

"Sure you don't want a ride? How'll you get back?"

"I'll just wander around awhile and then hop a bus. See you later, buddy."

He walked back to Euclid and then west again toward the Terminal Tower. After a few blocks he entered an office building with a bank of telephones along one wall of a large lobby. He stepped into a booth, closed the door and dialed a number.

After two rings a raspy voice said, "Brown Enterprises, Squillini speaking."

"Romeo, this is Vince. I got something. A jewelry salesman at seven-thirty tonight outside Rivers Jewelry Store on Euclid."

"I dunno, kid. They usually carry a bunch of junk."

"This one's good, I'm pretty sure."

"Hold on a second." Vince was aware of a hand-over-mouthpiece conversation and then, "You really think it's something worthwhile, kid?"

"Yeah, I do."

"Okay, then. Fill me in."

Vince talked a minute and then Squillini said, "Okay, kid, we'll take care of it. Make sure you're in public from about seven to eight. Have lots of people around you, Vince."

"Sure, Romeo."

Squillini dropped the phone and turned to a large man in a maroon dressing gown. "I dunno, Digger," he said. "Maybe it's something and maybe it's not."

The large man looked up from his breakfast and newspaper. He removed gold-rimmed glasses and ran a hand through salt-and-pepper hair. "It's worth a shot," he said. "Set it up."

Squillini lit a cigarette, thought for a moment and then picked up the phone again. When it was answered he said, "Ted, I gotta job for tonight. Come on down and bring Cardona."

Squillini jabbed a finger against the receiver button. When he heard the tone he dialed another number. "Frank Jablecnik," he said and then, after a pause, "Don't gimme none a that crap, just get him." A longer pause and then, "Frankie, you better wise up that guy that answered. This is Romeo. I need wheels for an hour at seven tonight. Nothing fancy. You and Lou handle it. Drop it off to Ted and Rocky at Euclid and Shaw. Seven o'clock."

He hung up and looked at the other man again. "Ted Friedlander and Rocky Cardona are coming over. Jablecnik and Petri are gonna take care of the car."

Digger Brown nodded and continued reading his newspaper.

After hanging up, Frankie Jablecnik walked to the rear of the body shop where Lou Petri was hammering a fender. "Romeo called," he said when Petri stopped work and looked up. Jablecnik took a small notebook from a shirt pocket under his coveralls, flipped pages, studied one a minute and said, "Got a job for seven tonight on the east side. How about that white Chevy at the tool and die place? When was the last time you checked it?"

"A week ago. It's okay from three to midnight."

Jablecnik nodded. "It'll do." He flipped pages again, saying, "Any ideas for a backup?"

"There's that blue '78 Ford at the same place or that old green Chevy on out at the X-ray plant. You got more in that book, too."

Jablecnik put the notebook back in his pocket. "That's enough, we're okay. Meet you at the bar at six."

The park bordered the street across from Rivers Jewelry Store so Bernie Friedman had no problem finding a parking space. There was a nip in the late fall air now that the sun was down so he put on the heavy overcoat again before going to the trunk for his cases. He had removed one case when a soft voice told him, "Put it back in for now, pal, and get in the car."

The rubber mask was so natural looking that several seconds passed before Friedman realized the man was wearing one. He knew at once what the hard object pressed against his side was. He replaced the case, closed the trunk and then with shaking fingers unlocked the door and slid behind the wheel.

"Unlock the other one," the soft voice commanded and Friedman did. Another man opened it and climbed in beside him. He, too, wore a lifelike rubber mask and had a gun.

The first man walked to a car parked a short distance ahead, entered it and pulled from the curb. "Follow him," said the man seated next to Friedman.

The two cars turned in at the park entrance. After a hundred yards the white Chevrolet in the lead drew to the side of the road and Friedman stopped behind it. The three men got out and the cases of merchandise were quickly transferred to the Chevrolet.

When the switch was completed the soft-voiced man walked to where Friedman cowered against the door of his car. He nodded toward a grove of trees and said, "Walk over there."

Friedman, his breathing labored, whispered, "Don't hurt me. Please don't hurt me."

The soft-voiced man laughed quietly. When they were under the trees he said, "Take off your clothes. Everything but your shorts."

"No, please —"

"Take 'em off. Fast." The voice, still soft, now was harsh, too. Friedman did as he was told. When he stood shivering in his shorts the other man scooped the clothes from the ground, removed the keys from a pocket and walked back to Friedman's car. He threw the clothes inside, locked both doors, dropped the keys in the trunk and slammed the lid. The two men got in the white Chevy and drove away.

A startled motorist taking a shortcut through the park a few minutes later speeded up when he saw a man clad in only polka-dot shorts standing beside the road waving both arms. Another weirdo, the driver thought. He stopped at the first phone booth and called the police. The two officers in a squad car that arrived after ten minutes found Bernie Friedman beating against the window of his car with a rock far too small for the job.

Casey stood in the doorway of the investigators room. His eyes roved from face to face, finally settled on Foley's. Foley stared back. Casey said, "Busy, Ferg?"

"Just winding up an insurance job."

Casey twitched his head a little. "Come on, then."

Foley gathered his papers together and got up. He followed the agency manager to his private office. When they were settled in chairs Foley asked, "What is it?"

"A jewel robbery. Did you see it in the paper?"

"The salesman? Yes, I saw it."

"We have to check it out."

A member of the Jewelers Protective Association?"

"I don't know yet. Whether he is or not, we have to report to them on it."

Foley nodded. "I had forgotten."

Casey took a cigar from his jacket pocket. "What's left to do on the insurance job?"

"Just talk to the subject."

Casey rolled the tip of the fat cigar between his lips. He removed it from his mouth and studied the result. "What part of town?"

"East off Euclid near Eddy Road."

"Good." Casey handed Foley a cutting from the *Plain Dealer*. "This is all I can give you right now. I'll get one of the girls to make out an assignment sheet later. Work it in with the other." He struck a match, held the flame a little below the cigar, puffed rapidly and then exhaled a cloud of yellowish smoke. "Any questions?"

Foley shrugged. "How much time?"

"Take the rest of the day. After that we'll see what develops."

Foley stood up. "Want me to check in after lunch?"

"Yeah, give me a call. Maybe we'll have more to go on by then."

Foley had little heart for the insurance job. He thought about it as he drove east on Euclid. He had ripped the woman's story apart so easily. A five minute walk from Wellington's National Detective agency on Public Square to the office of the Clerk of Courts. Ten minutes more checking files and he had all he needed. The rest would be window dressing.

Why hadn't the insurance company done that on its own? he wondered. It was possible that they had, of course. Perhaps all the company really wanted was an interview with the subject under pretext. An outsider would be needed for that.

Marie Gettis was suing the transit company for $50,000. She had been a standee on a bus that pulled from the curb with a severe lurch. Her right arm was broken in two places when she was hurled to the floor. The suit contended that she had suffered permanent loss of the use of her arm.

Beginning an insurance job by checking the court files was an agency routine. Sometimes it paid off. It had with Marie Gettis.

Four years before the accident on the bus she had been involved in another suit. In a crowded nightclub on a Saturday night she had been standing near the swinging door to the kitchen. A waiter carrying a loaded tray hurried through the door. They collided and both crashed to the floor along with the tray. Marie Gettis broke her right arm and the suit claimed she had lost the use of it permanently. The case was settled out of court shortly before the trial date.

How many times, Foley wondered, could you permanently lose the use of the same arm?

He had driven from the Clerk of Courts office to the nightclub. It was little more than a large tavern and just clean enough to keep its food and alcoholic beverage licenses. The owner recalled the incident immediately. Marie Gettis had been at fault, he said. She had been drunk and staggered in front of the waiter. Although nearly six years had gone by he remembered to the penny how much he had lost when the tray hit the floor.

Marie Gettis lived in an old apartment building three blocks from the nightclub. The neighborhood had been steadily decaying for thirty years or more. Spacious houses, formerly occupied by reasonably well-to-do families, had been converted to small efficiency units. Scattered among them were three- and four-story brick apartments that once, long ago, had been fashionable. Signs in front of shabby business places proclaimed that easy credit was available inside. The streets were littered and foul smelling. Mangy dogs and scrawny, mean-eyed cats prowled the alleys and back lots.

Foley had posed as a credit investigator while making the required check of the neighborhood. Statements from at least three persons had to be included in his report. From the brief interviews he formed a mental picture of Marie Gettis. A cheerful, friendly woman in her early forties. Always willing to help when someone was in need of it.

Deserted years ago, according to the neighbors, by a rodent of a husband.

She had been out the previous afternoon. Now Foley had to return, take a chance that she might be on guard because someone told her a man had been around checking on her. In this case it didn't really matter. In some it did and then he would have talked to the subject first. Seeing Marie Gettis was only a formality, something he was doing merely to satisfy one more requirement of the assignment.

Foley parked a block from her apartment. He put the raincoat and hat he had worn the day before in the trunk. He sorted through a box containing a variety of articles that could alter his appearance a little and picked out a pair of dimestore eyeglasses with lenses of clear glass. A sharp-eyed neighbor might recognize him as the credit investigator of the previous afternoon but he would go ahead and take his chances. The job didn't warrant sending out a second man to interview the subject.

Foley rigged a white sling that was in need of laundering so that it fit his right arm. A clipboard holding a stack of printed survey forms completed his props for the pretext. It was called roping and he was an expert at it.

He walked quietly along the dim hallway and knocked softly on the door of the woman's apartment, hoping the people he had talked to the day before wouldn't hear him, open their doors a crack and peek out.

Marie Gettis opened her own door no more than six inches. She stood behind it, peering around its edge in the defensive way that people do in such neighborhoods.

Foley fumbled with the clipboard and smiled. "Hello," he said. "I wonder if you could help me? I'm making a recreational survey of the area. It'll only take a minute." He smiled again, a pleading, little-boy smile.

She smiled back at him. "I'll try." She swung the door wide. "Come on in."

Foley looked around at the worn furnishings and faded wallpaper. "Nice place," he said. "Comfortable."

She wrinkled her nose. "It's not much but it's home." Then she laughed a little, patted her hair and waved him to a chair at a large, round table that was all that separated the living area from the kitchenette.

He struggled to get the clipboard in position, took a pen from his jacket pocket with his left hand and carefully placed it in his right one. He sighed as though the effort had tired him.

She nodded toward the sling. "What happened?"

Foley grinned sheepishly. "Fell off a ladder a month ago."

"You act like it still hurts."

He shrugged. "Not much. Mainly it's the inconvenience. I'm beginning to wonder if it's ever going to heal right."

She laughed again. "Don't worry, it will. Look at this one. It's been broken twice and it's as good as new." She maneuvered her right arm to show him it was.

Foley sighed, inwardly this time so she wasn't aware. Why did she have to be so cooperative? Why were people so quick to let their guard down with him? He almost wished the arm hung uselessly at her side or was stiff and contorted. He liked her. He would rather be able to report that she was deserving of a large settlement. Obviously life had dealt her some hard blows but still she managed to be pleasant. Optimistic, even. His job would be easier if she were belligerent.

"Care for a cup of coffee?"

He started to say no, saw the almost eager look on her face and instead said, "That would be good." She didn't receive many visitors, he decided. To her it was a special occasion.

He watched her put a spoonful of instant coffee in two cups and add hot water from a kettle. She set the cups on a tray and then took a carton of milk from the refrigerator, poured a little into a small pitcher with pale roses on its side and put it and a matching sugar bowl beside the cups. She placed several donuts taken from a plastic bag on a plate and then carried the tray to the table.

Foley drank his coffee black but he put a little cream and a little sugar in his cup. Why had he done that? he wondered. He wasn't hungry but he ate a donut anyway. They talked a while. When his cup was empty Foley picked up the pen again and filled in the questionnaire. As he left she stood in the doorway and said, "Now don't worry, that arm will be fine." He smiled back at her.

Light rain fell from a low gray sky. Foley dropped the sling and eyeglasses in the trunk of his car, retrieved his raincoat and hat. The roping had left him with an empty feeling in the pit of his stomach. Some insurance jobs affected him that way. Marie Gettis, he thought, would gladly have settled for her medical expenses and enough more to cover her time off work. An ambulance chaser had talked her into trying for the big score. The lawyer would keep half for himself, of course.

Fog began drifting in off the lake as he drove toward the central police station. Red, green and amber halos ringed the traffic lights and his tires sang a dismal tune on the wet pavement. Gloom settled over him as the gray mist enveloped the city. What would Marie Gettis receive after his report was filed? he wondered.

He was told Lieutenant Begley was handling the jewel robbery. Foley found him in a hallway talking to another detective. He stood a few feet away until Begley turned to him.

"The jewelry salesman, right?" Begley said.

Foley nodded. "Anything on it?"

Begley shrugged, scowling. "Everything and nothing. Come on, I'll fill you in."

Foley followed him to a desk in one corner of a squad room. Begley nodded toward a chair and slumped in another behind the desk. "Ever hear of a guy named Vince Levandowski?" he asked.

"Sounds a little familiar."

"A tall, blond kid about twenty-six or -seven. Carries a gun for the Glenwood Gang."
"He did it?"

Begley shook his head. "No. He was at a party. Must have been two dozen people there. Levandowski did everything but a song and dance routine to attract attention while the robbery was going on."

" So how does he fit in? "

"Let me ask you one, Ferg. Suppose you're a jeweler and you're going to a wholesaler to pick up stock. Would you take an armed robber with you?"

Foley chuckled. "Maybe, if I didn't have money to pay for it. You mean that's what happened?"

Begley nodded. "Bruce Rivers took Levandowski along to the Garfield Building yesterday morning. They ran into Friedman, the salesman, and he told Rivers he would be out at seven-thirty last night. You can guess what happened after that."
"How much did they get?"

"Friedman claims it had a retail value of $150,000. He says it's insured for fifty." Begley chewed the end off a cigar and spit it into a wastebasket. "I never have much faith in what people tell me after they've been robbed. Inflation isn't in the same ball game with the way things jump in value once they've been stolen."

"So where do you stand?"

"We're finished, unless something new develops and I don't think it will. Levandowski's down the hall right now but we'll have to turn him loose. We'll keep checking the fences but it won't lead to anything."

"How did Levandowski happen to be with Rivers?"

"They grew up together in Glenwood. Levandowski just happened to drop by the store."

"Think Rivers was in on it?"

Begley shook his head. No, it was pure coincidence. A helluva dumb play on Rivers' part but that was all. Levandowski passed the word to Digger Brown and one of the inner circle set it up. Probably Rick McCarthy or Romeo Squillini. A couple of their car specialists took one off a factory lot and turned it over to the two guys who did the job. They handed the jewels over to somebody else and ditched the car on Shaw just off Euclid.

"The salesman says one of the gunmen was a big guy with a soft, soothing voice. I'd bet my shirt it was Ted Friedlander but there's no way in hell to hang it on him. He claims he was shopping at a discount store all evening and his wife backs him up, naturally. A couple of clerks who know him say Friedlander was in the store for a long time but they can't pinpoint just when it was. There's just no way we could get a conviction."

Foley tapped his fingers together, studied Begley through a haze of cigar smoke. "So that's it?"

"Right. We'll file it away along with a cabinet full of other Glenwood Gang jobs. Knowing what happened and doing something about it are two different things."

"Are you saying you never make an arrest out of the Glenwood Gang?"

"No, Ferg, you know we do. But not often and then it's usually when a couple of them decide to freelance. A few months ago they got Levandowski and some hotshot out of Pittsburgh for holding up an all-night food store in East Liverpool. Caught 'em before they got out of town and the clerk made positive identifications. A few days ago when they were preparing for trial he decided he wasn't so sure after all so they ended up dropping the charges."

"What happened?"

Begley shrugged his shoulders. "Who knows? Somebody probably leaned on him or slipped him a few bucks. Who knows?"

"Digger Brown?"

"Not personally, you can be sure of that. Probably one of the Glenwood bunch or maybe somebody out of Pittsburgh. They accept serving time now and then as an occupational hazard but that doesn't mean they won't try to prevent it when they can. Brown doesn't like having too many of them out of circulation, it can slow up his operation."

Foley grinned and shook his head. He stood up and said, "I'll have to go through the motions. I'll let you know if I run across anything."

"You won't." Begley got up, too. "Want to see Levandowski before you go?"

"Sure."

Foley followed Begley back to the hallway and on to a small interrogation room. A detective was seated at one side of a table. Across from him a husky young man slouched in a chair, trimming his fingernails.

"Well, Vince," Begley said, "are you ready to tell us about it?"

Levandowski grinned. "Tell you what, lieutenant? I was partying last night. You know it, you checked it out."

"Who'd you tell about running into the salesman with Rivers?"

Levandowski raised his brows and held up his palms. "Nobody, lieutenant. I never gave it another thought."

"Okay, Vince, have it your way." Begley scowled at him. "Until another day, anyway. Go ahead, take off."

"Thanks, lieutenant." Levandowski grinned again and leisurely got out of his chair. "Sorry I can't help you but like I said, I was partying."

Begley continued to scowl. "We'll be seeing you again, Vince. Keep it in mind."

"Always a pleasure to talk to you, lieutenant." Still grinning, Levandowski walked out.

Begley turned to Foley. "Good luck, Ferg. Hope the J.P.A. isn't counting on an arrest."

Foley smiled. "They just like to keep tabs. Thanks, Herb." He followed Levandowski down the hall.

Talking to Rivers at the jewelry store turned up nothing new. Neither did interviewing other businessmen along the street or looking over the scene of the robbery in the park. Downtown again, Foley went to a small grille on East Ninth for lunch. The food was passable and the service impersonal, a good place to think undisturbed. He patronized the grille half a dozen times a month and always was greeted as a total stranger. He reviewed the morning over a corned beef sandwich and coffee.

What did he know? As Begley said, everything and nothing. What could he do? Talk to the salesman. Write out a report. Forget it. If it were a TV show he would find a way to break it wide open. He could see no way to do it. He might, provided someone was willing to pay for a lengthy undercover job. That could take months. No one would pay but even if someone would, he couldn't do it personally. He was known to some members of the Glenwood Gang, Levandowski included now. His cover wouldn't hold, not even for a day.

The rain had stopped so he walked the few blocks to Friedman's hotel. It was a cheap walk-up over a pawn shop and surplus store. There was no lobby, just a desk on the second floor. The neighborhood was a bad one.

After settling in a chair in Friedman's room, Foley said, "Seems like a strange place for a jewelry salesman to stay."

"For eighteen years I have," Friedman replied. "As long as I have been coming to Cleveland."

"It's a miracle you haven't been robbed right here."

"No trouble. Ever."

Foley shrugged. Friedman was red-eyed, tense. He hasn't slept, Foley thought. A pathetic man. A failure. A lifetime spent on the fringes of a lucrative business. A nervous person by nature and he would be worse now. The robbery would leave permanent scars. His life, no bargain to begin with, would never be quite the same again.

The interview was brief. Foley learned a few things that

Begley hadn't mentioned. Nothing of importance, just minor details to pad out his report. The undernourished salesman needed reassurance. Foley could think of nothing to say that might help him. He left Friedman standing at the window in trousers and undershirt, staring at the traffic below.

Foley called Casey from a phone booth. "Come on in, Ferg," the agency manager said. "Something's come up. The insurance company's been contacted and is going to buy back the jewels."

"How did they know who carried the insurance?"

"I have no idea. Come on in and we'll discuss it."

When Foley finished his story Casey leaned back, put one foot on his desk and lit a fresh cigar. When it was burning to his satisfaction he stroked his pencil-line mustache, chuckled and said, "Remind me not to call on Bruce Rivers when I need someone to do a little heavy thinking."

Foley flipped his notebook shut. "Too bad they can't charge him with contributory negligence. His stupidity could have gotten someone killed."

"It's too late now to worry about that part of it. By the way, who do you know in the Glenwood Gang?"

"I don't really know any of them. I have a nodding acquaintanceship with a few. Why?"

"We're going to handle the exchange for the insurance company. I should say *you* are. The contact man specified you when the arrangements were made."

"Foley frowned. "Why me, I wonder? That's strange."

"I don't think so. They want someone they'll recognize."

"You're right, I guess. When and where?"

"They'll call at five o'clock and tell you. Someone from the insurance company will drop the money off here in a little while." "How much?"

"Twenty-five thousand."

Foley whistled. "I'd better call Lieutenant Begley," he said.

"I've already handled it. He'll be standing by for a call. You've got a couple of hours so you might as well work on your reports."

The phone rang at one minute after five. Foley and Casey picked up extensions simultaneously. "Leave right now," a muffled voice said. "You've got two minutes to hit the street. Walk around Public Square past the cathedral and then south. Keep walking until you're contacted."

Foley picked up the briefcase containing the money and Casey said, "I'll phone Begley."

Ten seconds remained of the two minutes when Foley stepped from the revolving door onto the sidewalk. A car was parked in the loading zone in front of the building and three sample cases were on the sidewalk beside it.

"Over here, Foley," a man called from the car. The rubber masks the man and the driver were wearing were so lifelike that Foley at first was unaware they were masks at all.

"There's the stuff," the man said. "Let's have the briefcase."

"Don't you want to count it?" Foley asked. It was happening too fast but that didn't really surprise him.

The man in the car laughed hoarsely. "We trust you."

"How do I know the jewels are all here?"

"You know damn well they are. Now give me the case."

Foley handed it in the window and the car pulled away. He noted the license number, picked up the cases and struggled back through the revolving door.

Casey looked up in surprise. "You back already? God, you haven't been gone five minutes."

"They were waiting right outside the door. Call Begley for me. I got the license number, for all the good it'll do."

Begley called back a few minutes after seven. "No dice, Ferg," he said. "The car was stolen out at the X-ray plant. The owner was working, didn't know it was gone. The guys in the car going out to talk to him spotted it parked a block away before they even got there."

Well, Foley thought after hanging up, it figured. Still, until it had been checked out, there was a ray of hope. Now there wasn't.

Casey opened the door of the investigators room a few minutes later. "You still here, Ferg?" he said. "Better call it a day."

Foley nodded. "Yeah, it's been a dandy."

Casey laughed. " So you want to be a private eye."

"Sometimes I wonder why. I've been trying to separate the

winners and losers. So far I haven't had any luck."

Casey sat down across the table from him. "Forget it, Ferg. You can't figure things like that out. You've been around long enough to know it, too. Drop it and let's get a drink and something to eat."

'The jewelry salesman," Foley said. "Friedman, he's a loser. He'll never really get over it."

Casey shook his head. "Forget that angle if you're going to be crazy enough to try and sort it out. He's getting his stock back so he'll come out even."

"Marie Gettis, then. She's a loser."

"The woman with the insurance claim? Hell, she'll still get about three thousand. So she splits it with her lawyer and they each have fifteen hundred. Not big winners but still winners."

Foley twitched his shoulders. "So I guess that leaves the insurance companies."

Casey laughed and shook his head again. "The insurance companies, you've got to be kidding. The one stood to lose at least ten thousand on the insurance claim. Maybe as much as twenty-five. They're seven thousand ahead, minimum. The other would have had to hand the jewelry salesman fifty thou so they're twenty-five to the good. Anyway you look at it they're both winners."

Foley smiled. "You're right, I suppose. The Glenwood Gang is richer by twenty-five thousand, too."

Casey nodded. "Right. Say a thousand to each of the car artists and a couple to the ones who pulled the robbery. That's one, two, four, six thousand. Probably a couple to Levandowski and a thousand apiece to the two who made the exchange. That adds up to ten thousand and leaves fifteen for Digger Brown's kitty. If they had fenced the stuff they would have gotten about ten per cent so they're ten thousand ahead."

"The agency made a little money so I guess everybody's a winner."

"The agency made damn good money for handling the exchange. How much did you make, Ferg, including a couple of hours on the insurance job yesterday?"

Foley ran the figures through his mind. "About seventy-five dollars."

Casey stood up, grinning. "There's your answer. You're the loser. Come on, let's get that drink."

SECOND CHANCE

I watch her from across the room. Pretending to sip coffee, busying myself with lighting a cigarette, but always watching.

Ten years haven't changed her much. Still petite, still vivacious in a subdued way. Some of the other girls – women, now – have changed considerably. Not just the inevitable differences; new hair styles, and an added inch or two at the waist, the first hint of lines in skin that had been creamy smooth. Those changes are of no importance. The ones that matter are the signs of hurt or despair, of disillusionment or, worst of all, acceptance. They show in the eyes and around the mouth, can't be concealed by makeup or a new dress or a trip to a hair stylist.

But Jenny looks the same. Her brown hair isn't shoulder length and silky now, its frizzy curls that toss and bob when she turns her head or leans back to study a new arrival, then smile in delayed recognition. Her skirt falls just below her knees, not three inches above them anymore. Her cheeks may not be quite so full but still she looks the same. Except for the gold band on the third finger of her left hand.

She hasn't seen me sitting just beyond the glow of the crystal chandelier that lights all but the outer reaches of the ballroom. Jenny was never a pretender. If she had known I was coming she would have been watching for me and if she knew I was here she would smile her dimpled smile, wave, and come over. But no one knew I was coming and few realized or care that I am here. Soon someone will tell her, though, and that's why I'm watching now, before she knows. Jenny was never a pretender but having me around would make a difference.

A man who has been standing at the makeshift bar in one corner walks to her table and sits down, blocking my view of her. He is sullen, bored with the people he doesn't know, and his resentment shows. His back is to me but I can see it in the set of his shoulders, the way he holds his head.

Three others are at the table with me. People I once knew, or thought I did, but being with them now means being alone. I look around the long, rectangular room, remembering it from long ago. On prom night the woodwork around the doors and windows had been polished and glowing. Now it has been painted white and the walls are pink. Only the chandelier remains unspoiled.

Some faces are familiar but many are not. Wives or husbands tied to the class of '73 but a little ill at ease because they are outsiders, not really a part of all this. Most are content to sit or stand quietly, smiling politely when forced to meet yet another person they never heard of, don't really care to know, will forget in two minutes. Still smiling, and trying to make it an understanding smile, when told some anecdote that is amusing only to those who were a part of it. Listening with the same pasted-on smile as each new introduction is followed by, "This is the one I told you . . ." You should have been there when . . ." or something similar.

Even some of the class members have a glassy-eyed look that says they are wondering why they ever let themselves in for something like this, something that isn't at all the way they thought it would be. They are pleasant enough when someone accosts them gushing. "Why, it's . . .", but approach no one themselves, aside from the bartender.

Others seem to be enjoying themselves, though, acting as self-appointed hosts or hostesses. They scurry about the room, pausing here and there for a breathless word, a quick laugh. Latecomers are descended upon, taken by the elbow and hurried to some group to be greeted by hugs or handshakes, back-slapping or gales of laughter.

And of course a few, most of them men, seem compelled to impress old classmates with their success. The more ostentatious they are or the noisier they are the more it comes across that they aren't doing well at all.

Seeing them together again I realize that I never really knew any of them, just their names and their faces. Aside from Jenny. I knew Jenny. Not the others, though, because I was never a part of anything back then. I went to class, went to basketball games, sometimes went to a dance or party, but I wasn't actually a part of any of it, a real participant. That was how I wanted it.

My glass is empty and I have heard enough of the silly prattle, the excited whispering of the others at the table. Enough of the pointing and the "Look, isn't that . . .", and, "Who do you suppose that woman is with him? Surely he wouldn't . . ." When someone who has been to the bar too often throws his arm over the shoulder of the man next to him and starts singing, "Midland Central, our Midland Central . . .," I murmur an excuse that no one seems to notice and go to the bar myself.

They are lined up two deep so I stand and wait my turn at one end where I won't feel hemmed in. I exchange a few nods and smiles, even a couple of handshakes, but nothing more. Eventually one of the harried men behind the bar pours equal amounts of vodka and club soda into a glass and hands it to me in exchange for three dollar bills. I stir it myself, something he didn't bother to do.

Suddenly I am aware that Jenny is beside me. The hint of gardenia, different on her than anyone else, would have told me anywhere. I turn and she is standing close, smiling up at me. And still she is the same. The little twinkle in her brown eyes, the white teeth just imperfect enough to look real.

All I say is, "Jenny." And all I do is touch her hand. A tentative touch quickly ended.

"How are you, Tom?" she asks.

How am I? How would I describe it? Exhilarated, somewhere in the clouds. Devastated, the ground pulled from under my feet. A record high, a new low, mixed together in something indescribable because Jenny's here again, but now she isn't mine.

"Fine, Jenny, just fine. How about you?"

"Fine, Tom." She lowers her eyes, then raises them again and the twinkle is gone. "I'm married, you know."

I look away and nod.

She laughs softly, a little uncomfortable. "Mrs. Brian McLeod," she says, and there is something in the way she says it that I don't understand. But she's not Jenny Williams anymore, she's Jenny McLeod. Mrs. Brian McLeod.

A band has begun to play, but not a song from '73. Something quieter, more sentimental, from a generation before ours. A few couples are already on the floor.

"Dance, Jenny?" She smiles again and I know it means yes.

For a while I'm content just holding her again, lost somewhere in the only world I ever wanted. A world I might have had, tried to have, but fumbled away. But all that is forgotten for a moment or two. Then Jenny looks up at me and says, "Where did you go, Tom?"

Why lie about it, why pretend? I look deep into her brown eyes and say, "To prison."

They change, of course. The twinkle is gone again but she doesn't turn them away. They pose a question, though, but I know she'll never ask it, never put it into words. That wouldn't be Jenny's way. So I tell her, "Armed robbery. A bank, and the man with me killed a guard. I was tried for murder, too, but acquitted. I served eight years at Rahway." She waits a little, then says. "You must have needed the money badly."

For you, Jenny, I think to myself. But how like you to see it from my point of view rather than condemn or moralize. And the bank hadn't been the first because I wanted lots of money. A job in one of the factories, a weekly pay check, that wasn't enough for you, Jenny. You were the daughter of a shop worker but I didn't want you to be the wife of one. I had bigger things in mind. Real money and all it could do. Now I have it, stashed away in different places they've never been able to find, but I don't have you.

She looks at me strangely, seems to peer into the darkest recesses of my mind, and too late I realize why. She has felt the hard bulge under my left arm and thinks I haven't changed. But I have, at least for a while. The gun in the special pocket sewn into my jacket is for protection from my own kind, the few who also know the money is out there somewhere and might decide they want it for themselves.

Of course Jenny doesn't know that and yet she doesn't seem disturbed. She is smiling again, smiling with her mouth and eyes. We glide around the floor quietly for a few moments, continuing when the orchestra goes on to a second number, and a third.

Then Jenny asks, "Are you staying here at the hotel?" And I tell her that I am. "So are we," she says. "We live in town but I thought it would be more fun to have a room at the hotel."

"Do you have children?" I ask. Without preface the question once asked seems too blunt, too personal. I am pleased, though, when she shakes her head. But I look at her, puzzled for a moment, when she says, "Thank God."

Then I understand. In a way that pleases me, too. But it saddens me as well because I have always wanted Jenny to be happy. I want that more than anything else, even more than I want her for my own.

"Problems?" I ask, and she lowers her head for a moment, then turns slowly until her eyes focus on her right arm. Mine follow and I see two faint bruises, barely visible above the right elbow. For an instant anger surges inside me, then I control it, force myself to remain detached. It's her business, not mine, unless she chooses to make it so.

The music stops and we walk together back to the bar. We talk a little, small talk about the old days while I try to attract a bartender. I turn though, when someone says, "An old flame, Jenny?"

It's the sullen man who was at her table earlier. He is about my size and weight, even looks a little like me. At close range, however, there is an air of timidity about him and a petulant look in his eyes. I've met his type before, the kind who bow and scrape to those above them but are mean and petty when dealing with those of lesser authority. To him, that would mean Jenny.

As she introduces us Jenny, uncharacteristically, seems flustered, unsure of herself. He smiles from one side of his mouth but it isn't genuine. I reach out and grip his hand, find it flaccid and unresponsive.

But alcohol has made him bold and loosened his tongue. Even so he doesn't meet my eyes when he says, "So you're the old lover my wife is always hankering after?" He's loud and heads turn.

There is nothing to say in reply. I stare at him while Jenny touches his arm and whispers, "Please, Brian."

He brushes her hand away, pretending to be surprised. "Oh, I'm sorry." he says mockingly. "I didn't realize it was supposed to be a secret." He moves his head to encompass the room in what he's saying. "I'm afraid it's out of the bag, though. Everybody's saying how nice it is to see the ex-lovers together again."

The room is quiet, he has gained everyone's attention. Jenny has a waxen look. I can feel the anger rising again. "Just how do you mean that?" I ask him. Jenny turns to me, distressed, and shakes her head.

He is enjoying the scene he has created. It's his big moment, a new experience for him, so he basks in the spotlight and relishes her discomfort. "How do I mean it?" he mimics. "I mean it in every sense the term implies." Then, to Jenny, "But I shouldn't have believed, my dear, that you'd flaunt your old bedmates in public this way."

Even as I reach out, grab the front of his shirt and pull him, close to me, I realize he knows the lie of what he has said better than anyone else and that I am only doing what he wants, adding to Jenny's humiliation. Fear flickers in his eyes but he has gone too far to stop now. He lashes out at me but his punch is weak and ineffective, easily blocked with my free arm. I draw back to retaliate but Jenny locks both hands around my wrist. "No, Tom, no." she says pleadingly. "Please, just go now. No more, please."

For a moment I stay poised, wanting to strike back, shaken to see her so dismayed. Then I lower my arm and loosen my grip, turn and walk quickly away.

I go straight to my room, climbing the two flights of stairs rather than wait for the elevator. I take off my tie and shoes, hang my jacket over the back of a chair, and stretch out on the bed.

Thinking that I shouldn't have come, should have had the sense to stay away, doesn't help because being aware of it doesn't eradicate the pain I have inflicted on Jenny. I have hurt her, the one thing above all else that I never wanted to do. For several hours I try to think of a way to make it up to her, to help her straighten out her life. No answers are forthcoming and mixing an occasional drink from the bottles on the dresser doesn't provide any.

A soft tapping on the door jars me from the funk I have been in. I glance at my watch and it's past midnight. When I open the door, Jenny is standing there. We look at each other for several seconds and I can see she has been crying. I step aside, and when the door has closed behind her we embrace. This may only complicate her situation, I think to myself, but she wants to talk so I don't discourage her. She sits down, sniffling a little, while I mix two drinks. When I turn back to her she is smiling, even with her eyes.

We talk for an hour. She does most of it, telling me the details of her life but never complaining, rationalizing instead, making excuses for him. But that would be Jenny's way. We make no attempt to arrive at a solution but when she says she must leave it's with the promise that we will meet again. Although neither of us puts it into words, there is an understanding between us that something will be done to get her life on track again.

Another hour passes before I finally fall into a fitful sleep. Light streams in the open window when the crashing in of the door jerks me suddenly awake. Two men with guns in hand confront me. One is in uniform.

"Thomas Stapleton?" the other says. I nod, then sit quietly as he recites my rights from memory.

I think of the gun in the jacket draped over the chair where Jenny sat earlier. If they find it, which they surely will, it will be enough to send me back to prison. But while I am still trying to make some sense of what is happening in my sleep-fogged mind, another man in street clothes comes in. He walks to the side of the bed and holds out a plastic bag containing an object. "Is this your gun?" he asks.

I look at it and nod again. "Where did you get it?"

"From a trash container two floors up. Just down the hall from where it was used to kill a man."

"Brian McLeod?"

"You should know."

"How did you know it was mine?"

We heard about your fight with him earlier, among other things. And we've checked your record so no need to play games about that."

I study him, but really am studying what he has said. When I have it straight in my mind I say. "I don't like games. I guess you've got it figured."

We talk a while, then they tell me to get dressed. While I button my shirt the detective who broke in the door stares at me, shaking his head. "It doesn't add up," he says. "A pro like you tossing a gun away just thirty feet from where he used it."

I shrug my shoulders. "I guess you boys were sharper than I thought."

He shakes his head again. "I don't think so. You know if you stick to this story you may not get a second chance."

He's right, I won't get a second chance. But Jenny will.

THE FOURTH FRIDAY

He sat staring at her photograph, his eyes like open windows letting the sickness of his mind escape into the room. They were taking her away from him. Pushing him aside like you'd kick an old pair of shoes to the back of the closet.

It was unfair. A conspiracy. He was the one who had worshipped her as long as he could remember. From the time she had been what, ten or eleven? He thought back, matching dates with events. No, she had been only nine. The others had made over her, placed her on a pedestal, taken their places as members of her court, but he was the one who realized she was a goddess, the only one who appreciated just how unique she really was. And they had always been so close, the two of them.

But now they had made her all but forget he existed. A castoff with no place in the excitement, the frantic preparations and, worst of all, the sickening adulation of the latecomer. The Chosen One. Prince Charming. The Intruder.

It had happened so fast. Their little get-together, the sudden unexpected announcement, the plans that didn't include him. They had influenced her, talked her into doing this, he knew that. And all so quickly so he wouldn't have time to do anything about it. Then, just to be certain, they had sealed her off from him. Always fluttering around her, giving him little opportunity to convince her how wrong it all was. The three weeks had sped by and now there were only three to go.

They had poisoned her mind but she had done nothing to prevent it. No, she had gone right along with them and that made it worse, made it hurt even more. If she had turned to him, asked him to send them away, it all would have been so different. Or if she told him it was a sacrifice she had to make, then he might have understood. But no, she was happy about it. They had done something to her and now she was no better than the rest.

And her patronizing manner, her newest way to hurt him. Patting his arm, smiling at him, telling him he looked so lost and forlorn. "Poor boy, you just feel left out of everything. But you want me to be happy, don't you? I won't forget about you, silly. No one can ever really take your place, you know that."

Lies, that's what they were. How could she be happy now? And no one take his place? That was the biggest lie of all. If it wasn't, why was she marrying The Intruder in three weeks?

He pulled the photo from its frame and held it up to the light, feverish eyes burning into it. Then he picked up a long, pointed knife and rotated it in his hand for a moment. Suddenly he lashed out at the photo, ripping it, tearing it with frenzied slashes until it fell to the desk in shreds. He had nicked his thumb and small beads of red dripped down on what had been her picture. He smiled then; a sick smile that went with his sick eyes. First blood, he thought. But not the last.

Patches of fog swirled in from the lake, white specters that formed halos around the lights along the drive and made the houses set well back from the street seem even farther away than they were. The sound of young women's laughter came from a cab as it stopped in front of one of the huge houses. A girl got out and another called, "Now don't forget, be ready early. We have a big day tomorrow."

"I won't," she answered, still laughing as she ran up the steps and along the walk toward the bright lights of the house, friendly rectangles of yellow in the mist. As she neared the door a hand shot out from the darkness of the shrubbery and grasped her wrist. She gave a little cry but then, when she realized who it was, exhaled and said, "Oh, it's you. You gave me a fright. What are — "

She stopped when she saw his eyes. Her own rounded as the knife was drawn from the folds of his cloak. "No — " she began but suddenly the hand left her wrist and was over her mouth. Light from a window glinted on the blade as it rose and descended, rose and descended.

Riley Cullan looked up from his desk when the door opened. "Superintendent," the secretary said, "the major would like to see you." He got up immediately and walked down the hallway to the door on which a bronze plaque read Major Ira Wellington. He knocked and was told to enter. When Cullan was settled in a chair the major said, "Riley, I have something here I want you to handle personally. I'm sure you've read about these murders. The two on the north side that the papers are playing up so much." He waved at a stack of newspapers on his desk. "It's revolting, the names they've coined for him. The Lake Shore Slasher. The Gold Coast Killer. My God, there's something depraved, almost ghoulish about it."

Cullan nodded. "But it sells papers. How does the agency come into it?"

"Henry Farmer, the father of the girl murdered last night, is an old friend of mine. He's distraught, of course, and isn't pleased with the way the police are handling the investigation. He wants the killer caught. He insisted that I come out but I'm seventy years old. I convinced him we need a young man on this."

Cullan smiled to himself. He had recently celebrated his fifty-fifth birthday. Apparently the major still thought of him as he had been thirty years earlier when he joined Wellington's National Detective Agency, a youth fresh from a military hospital.

Like most others in the neighborhood, the Farmer

residence was ostentatious. A big, towering sandstone building that might have been an armory or, with bars on the windows, a prison. Sinister, Cullan thought, but maybe that was only because he knew what had taken place inside the night before.

"It was my fault," Henry Farmer said softly. "I'm to blame. When I had the fire escapes installed I thought it was a wise move, a safety precaution. I never dreamed someone could pull one down and then —" His voice trailed off but suddenly blared out again, "I want this madman caught!"

"We all do, Mr. Farmer," Cullan said quietly. "Tell me, did your daughter know the other girl, Lillian Myers?"

"Of course. They were close friends. But the police have gone over all this."

"Please bear with me, Mr. Farmer. Something new might occur to you. Had she seen Miss Myers recently?"

"A week ago last night. The night Lillian was — was murdered. Audrey was very upset. Of course we never dreamed — " His voice broke.

"Had anything unusual happened involving them recently? Something out of the ordinary. Did the two of them do anything, go anywhere— "

Henry Farmer waved a hand impatiently. "Nothing. Nothing at all. They were excited about the Telfare girl's wedding but it's the fourth one in their circle this season. Nothing unusual about that."

A young man seated in a chair near Farmer cleared his throat. "There was one thing, father. That house party you were so upset about when you returned from New York."

Cullan turned to Carl Farmer, younger brother of the latest victim. "What's this, now?"

"Nothing, really, but it upset father."

"Nothing!" the elder Farmer snapped. "You call four young ladies going off alone for a weekend in the country un-chaperoned *nothing*? Well, I don't. If your mother were alive she never would have permitted it."

The young man smiled bleakly. "Father, this is 1893. Girls do things like that all the time now. The servants were there, you know."

He looked at Cullan and cleared his throat again. "It was

Marcia Telfare's idea. A month ago the four of them went off on what you might call a soul-searching venture. In any event, they came back on a Sunday evening and the next day Marcia announced her engagement.

"Audrey was very secretive about it but still was dropping hints all over the place. Apparently Marcia couldn't make up her mind so they all gave their opinions, that sort of thing. Anyway, she decided to go ahead."

Cullan tapped the ends of his fingers together for a moment. "And you say there were four of them: your sister, Lillian Myers, Marcia Telfare and who else?"

"Jill Cosgrove."

The Cosgrove home was three blocks away on Astor Street. Its rear yard abutted that of the Telfare property on Lake Shore Drive. The Cosgroves called their residence a chateau but in Cullan's opinion it was just another of Chicago's cold, pretentious mansions. The family, shocked by the two murders, readily assembled in the drawing room at Cullan's request. There was only the young lady and her parents.

"Anything we can do sir, anything at all," the father blustered.

"But I don't know what it would be," the mother murmured. Her husband glared at her.

Jill Cosgrove leaned forward in her chair and fixed Cullan with a cold stare from red-rimmed eyes as if somehow he was responsible for the death of her friends. "First Lillian and now Audrey," she hissed. "It's so awful — " She began to weep.

Cullan waited a moment and then said, "Tell me about the weekend when the four of you went away. About a month ago, was it?"

"Four weeks today," she sobbed. "It was nothing. Marcia couldn't decide so we all went to their country place and talked it over. And now the wedding's only two weeks away and — "

"Two weeks?" Cullan said, surprised. "Isn't that rather fast?"

"Very," said Mrs. Cosgrove.

Her husband glowered at her again. "Quite understandable," he said pompously. "Business, you know. The young man – one of the Winfields of Boston and a good match – sails on the thirtieth for two years at the London office of the family firm. That's why Marcia had to decide one way or another without delay."

Cullan turned to Jill again. "Were – or are – there any other young men in Miss Telfare's life?"

She shook her head. "No." She frowned a little then and added, "Well, just Earl Maynard."

"Who is Earl Maynard?"

"An old — " Jill began.

But her father interrupted: "Family lived down the street until a few years ago. Went broke. The boy's still around Chicago but of course the Telfares would never allow . . . well, it was rather presumptuous of the young man to still call, to even think they might consider — "

"Oh, daddy!" Jill cried. "Why are you so – so stuffy? Earl's a fine, sensitive person."

Her father went, "Humph!"

Cullan stared at the girl. "Have you seen this Maynard recently?"

She shook her head. "Not since Marcia announced her engagement." Her voice trailed away toward the end. She looked contemplative.

"What is it?" Cullan asked.

She shook her head. "Oh, nothing."

"Tell me, please. It could be important."

She hesitated and then gave a little shrug. "Just that Marica said Earl was upset. Really angry."

"With her?"

"With all of us. He thought we talked her into marrying Teddy Winfield."

"Did you?"

Jill shook her head. "Marcia's too headstrong for that. Earl knows it; he was just upset. Marcia listens to people, but she makes up her own mind."

Cullan tapped his fingers on the arm of the chair for a few seconds. Then he stood up. "I don't want to alarm you or your parents, Miss Cosgrove, but I'm going to arrange for someone to stay with you temporarily."

146

"What!" Cosgrove bellowed. "You mean a guard? You think Jill's in danger?"

Cullan nodded. "Perhaps. We won't take any chances."

At police headquarters an hour later he summarized what he had learned to the detective in charge. He ended with, "It's imperative that we find this Maynard right away."

"Absolutely," the detective replied. "Sounds like he may be our man all right."

The Telfares agreed to see Cullan the following day although Joseph Telfare made it clear on the telephone that he was not accustomed to receiving private detectives, and certainly not on Sunday. "In view of the circumstances, though — " Just like Cosgrove and Farmer, Cullan thought. Big businessmen. Cast from the same mold.

The Telfare home was even more impressive than the others he had visited. Or repressive, to Cullan's thinking. A three-story monstrosity of Joliet marble with a turreted tower looming ominously above. Simon Culp, one of the agency's best young operatives, accompanied Cullan. The family was awaiting their arrival in a large room paneled in ebony and mahogany.

Marcia Telfare proved to be a striking brunette of twenty-three with just a touch of haughtiness in her eyes. Disturbed by the murder of her friends, thought Cullan, but displeased by her forced attendance at this gathering. Her mother also was an attractive woman and more assertive than her neighbor, Mrs. Cosgrove.

Joseph Telfare, while obviously sharing Cosgrove's and Farmer's contempt for all things not connected with making money, bore little physical resemblance to the others. He was thin, almost cadaverous, with angry, impatient eyes and a nervous habit of tugging at a small goatee.

His son, Marcus, an eighteen-year-old cursed with acne and a chin that was nearly non-existent, shook hands limply and then retired to an oversized chair in a corner.

147

The two men who completed the group didn't bother with the formalities. Frederick Boswick, a cousin, was a medical student at the university and had lived with the Telfares since the death of his parents in an accident several years earlier. He gave Cullan and Culp an informal wave of his hand but didn't bother to stand. Teddy Winfield, the future groom, a cold-eyed, stiff featured young man who Cullan disliked instantly, merely nodded curtly.

Joseph Telfare took charge, as was his custom. "Unfortunate as the deaths of the young ladies may be, superintendent," he said, "I fail to see how they involve us."

Cullan shrugged, "Maybe they don't. But there's a possibility they do so your cooperation is appreciated."

"Well I think you're on the wrong track completely," Marcia Telfare proclaimed loudly. Surprised, Cullan turned to her with the trace of a frown.

"How so?"

"Jill Cosgrove says you suspect Earl Maynard and that's ridiculous. He could no more kill anyone than – than I could."

"Have you seen the young man lately?"

"No. Not for more than a week. But that has nothing to do with it."

"But you were close at one time?"

Marcia shifted uncomfortably. "We've been friends since childhood, if that's what you mean."

Cullan leaned forward. "Did he have any reason to believe you were more than friends? Any understanding that — "

"Really, sir!" the senior Telfare interjected. "I don't see how this has any bearing on your investigation." He looked at his daughter and Marcia, blushing, glanced quickly at her fiance. Winfield, stone-faced, stared straight in front of him.

After a few seconds Cullan turned to Marcia again. "Did he?" he asked quietly.

She darted another look at Winfield. "I don't know. We were – were very close. Perhaps he – oh, I don't know."

"Do you know where he's living now?"

Marcia shook her head. "No. He had an apartment on Clark Street but" – her face glowed pink again – "when I

148

telephoned Tuesday they said he had moved."

Her mother frowned disapprovingly. "Really Marcia. You mean you called a young man's apartment?"

Marcia nodded defiantly. Cullan smiled to himself. Good girl, he thought.

The rest of the interview was uneventful. Marcia protested halfheartedly when told a guard would also be assigned to her but admitted she had a recent photo of Maynard. She turned it over to Cullan saying, "We exchanged pictures in the spring."

Cullan and Culp walked to the nearest trolley line. "What did you think of the Telfares?" Cullan asked.

Simon Culp, who held his superior a little in awe, didn't want to say the wrong thing. "Well, sir, they – I – that is — "

Cullan laughed. "I agree with your opinion." He handed Culp the photo. "Find him. Fast. Use as many operatives as you need."

It soon became apparent that ordering Maynard found was easier than running him to earth. The major summoned Cullan to his office again the following Friday morning. "I can't understand why young Culp hasn't turned him up, Riley," he said. "Maybe you should put someone else on it."

Cullan shook his head. "Culp is doing everything that could be done. He has three operatives working with him practically around the clock and the police have as many or more on it. It's a big city, major, and we're not even sure Maynard's still in it."

The major pulled one corner of his bristly white mustache. "Well it worries me, Riley. You're doing more than just looking for Maynard, I take it?"

Cullan nodded. "We've followed up every lead without result. I've also had men at every house in the neighborhood. They concentrated on servants, mainly. Sometimes they know more than the pompous windbags they work for."

"Cullan!" the major barked. "I belong to the same clubs as the people you're talking about and — " His frown faded and a smile threatened to take its place. "They are an insufferable bunch, aren't they?"

Cullan laughed but sobered quickly. "I don't like it either, major. It's Friday again, you know. Both murders have been on a Friday. We've assigned a woman operative to stay in both the Cosgrove and Telfare girls' rooms tonight and we'll have a man downstairs in each house." He stared out the window at the buildings on the other side of State Street for a moment. Then he shook his head slowly. "But I still don't like it."

Jill Cosgrove giggled. Trust Marcia to outwit the guards who had turned the two houses into prisons. How did she manage to get the note over here? She wondered. She picked it up and read it a second time.

"Jillsy – I must see you, lovey. I absolutely must! All these stupid wardens, you'd think we were criminals. Well, we can outfox them, can't we? Meet me at ten tonight in the summerhouse – you just won't believe what's happened! Don't call me, though. They even have spies on the telephone. Can you really imagine it? And burn this, too, as soon as you've read it. If it falls into their grubby hands I might be shot at sunrise! But we'll show them, won't we, sweetsy! Love, Marcy."

She giggled again. That was Marcia, all right. Not going to let a little thing like a few guards keep her down. Then unexpectedly a twinge of apprehension swept over her. She hurried to a desk in the corner of her bedroom and sorted through a pile of envelopes until she found the one she wanted. She removed the letter and held it and the note side by side. After a few seconds she laughed. The handwriting seemed identical to her. Why had she even questioned it? She walked to the fireplace and struck a match.

The woman had been waiting in the hall when Jill left the dining room. She was nice enough but, still, having someone right in your own bedroom like this . . .

"I have the most awful headache." Jill held the back of her hand against her forehead and moaned a little. The woman looked up from the book she was reading. "Please," Jill said, "go down and ask cook to fix me a potion. She'll know what I want."

150

"Well, I don't know," the woman drawled uncertainly.

"For heaven's sake!" Jill said with peevishness. "It won't take you a minute but if you won't do it I'll go myself." She headed for the door.

The woman put her book down. "All right, I'll go. But don't leave your bedroom. Promise?"

Jill gave her a gamine smile. As soon as the woman turned the corner of the hallway she dashed lightly down the servant stairway and slipped out the back door.

She stood for a moment, adjusting her eyes to the sudden blackness. A shiver traveled up and down her spine but she laughed to herself and thought: you big silly. It was dark, though, and she had to pick her way carefully among the bushes and trees. At last she saw the summer house in front of her. A shadowy figure was outlined in the doorway. She thought: "Oh, good! Marcia's here already." She rushed ahead.

Cullan hung up the phone and smashed his fist down on the table. "Damn!" Why had they let her out of their sight? He had told them that under no circumstances were they to leave her alone for even a second. And the poor, foolish girl. Why hadn't she listened to him? But don't blame her. Not now, not after what's happened. He stood up slowly, suddenly very tired.

When he reached the Cosgrove house he tried to console the weeping operative who had let the girl slip away. He had intended to reprimand her. Now he realized it would do no good. The responsibility had been his. It was he who had failed. He did what had to be done and then went home again. More weary, more discouraged than he ever could remember feeling.

Cullan returned the next day and went over it all from beginning to end. He took the female operative with him, had her run through exactly what transpired with him playing the part of Jill. The bedroom had been searched by the police but he went over it again. He found nothing pertinent until, while kneeling in front of the fireplace, a scrap of pink paper caught his eye. He removed it carefully. Only a corner remained unburned. On it he could see the word *we*.

How long had it been there? he wondered. Had Jill been lured to her death? What might have persuaded her to go outside? He ran the possibilities through his mind. He could think of only one that seemed likely: a note from Marcia Telfare.

Her eyes were swollen and webbed with threads of crimson when she came downstairs. "I'm sorry to disturb you, Miss Telfare," Cullan said. He held the scrap of paper out to her. "Do you have stationery like this?"

She studied it a few seconds and then looked at him quizzically. "It looks like mine. Why?"

"Did you write a note to Jill Cosgrove recently?"

She shook her head. "Why? Where did you get this?"

"From the fireplace in her bedroom. Look at the writing. Is it yours?"

She walked to the window and held it in the light. "It could be. It's so hard to tell. If there was more — "

Cullan nodded. "I know. Who has access to your stationery?"

"Why anyone in the house, I suppose. It's standard stationery, though. Marshall Field's carries it and I'm sure a number of other stores."

"Does Earl Maynard know your handwriting? Could he have an example of it in his possession?"

For a second her eyes smouldered but then she shrugged her shoulders. "I've written to him. He could have kept my letters, I suppose." She turned away momentarily. When she swung back around her eyes were blazing again. "You're implying that Earl wrote a note and got her to go to the summer house, aren't you?"

Cullan hesitated before answering. Then he nodded. "Yes, I think he may have. I believe someone did. The only thing I can think of that might have gotten her to go last night was a note she thought came from you."

Marcia sat down abruptly and put her hands over her face. "My God, that's awful. Poor, poor Jill." She looked up at him then and softly added, "But Earl wouldn't have written it."

When he reached the door Cullan looked back and said, "The wedding. Is it still on?"

She slowly nodded her head.

The days slipped by without developments. The stationery proved too common to trace. More men were added to the detail searching for Maynard but the result was the same. Cullan assigned two female and three male operatives to the Telfare house for the entire week. It was quiet there, too.

On Thursday he returned there himself to warn Marcia once more against going outside unescorted. He found her depressed, listless. Hardly the eager bride, he thought. Of course considering the circumstances it was understandable. But, he wondered, was it more than just the death of her friends? Could it also be the man she was marrying? If so, he could understand that, too.

The hours dragged endlessly on Friday. The wedding was at seven o'clock. Late in the afternoon Cullan started for the Telfare mansion. He had walked down only one flight of stairs when the secretary ran from the office and leaned over the railing.

"Superintendent!" she cried. "Superintendent, come back. Mr. Culp's on the telephone. They've caught him. They've caught Maynard!"

Cullan turned and took the steps two at a time. He listened to Culp's excited voice for several seconds and then interrupted: "Bring him in. Right away!" While he waited he couldn't recall just what Culp had said. Something about a tavern on Wentworth.

Earl Maynard was surprisingly sober for a man reeking of cheap whiskey. He and Cullan sized each other up like boxers waiting for the opening bell. Maynard needed a shave, a bath and clean clothes. He slouched in a chair eyeing Cullan sardonically. Culp stood at his shoulder and another operative was just inside the door.

Maynard spoke first. "I take it you're the chief of this monkey squad." He jerked his head toward Culp and the other operative. "Your strong-arm boys got me here, so now what?"

Cullan stared at him a few seconds longer. Then he said, "You didn't know we'd been looking for you for two weeks?"

153

"Why should I? I've been gone for three ."

"Where?"

"What business is it of yours?"

Anger surged through Cullan. "The death of three young women makes it everybody's business."

Maynard looked shocked. "What are you talking about?"

"The murders of Lillian Myers, Audrey Farmer and Jill Cosgrove."

Maynard jerked upright in his chair. The skin under and around his stubble of whiskers faded to a chalky white. Horror, tempered a little by disbelief, flickered in his eyes. He started to speak but had to swallow before he could. "Murdered?" he finally croaked.

Cullan tried to gauge the man's reaction. A good actor? An innocent man? Insane? There were people like that. Commit crimes but have no recollection of it. It was possible. After a moment he said, "Can you prove you weren't in Chicago the past three Friday nights?"

Maynard thought a few seconds. "The last two I can. Three weeks ago I was on a train." He hesitated again. "What you said about the murders, it's true then?"

Cullan nodded. "Where were you?"

"Pittsburgh. Visiting my parents. A dozen people can verify it."

Checking it will take time, Cullan thought. Suppose he's telling the truth? It would mean the killer is loose. Loose out there somewhere on a Friday night. The fourth Friday.

He looked at the operative by the door. "Telegraph the Pittsburgh office. Have them check it as quickly as possible and get right back to us." The man jotted down the name and address Maynard gave him and hurried from the room.

Cullan looked at his watch. Nearly six o'clock. An hour until the wedding. His eyes went to the window. Dark already. He felt empty inside. Something was wrong. He knew it. He wasn't sure why, but he knew it.

I've handled it wrong from the start, he thought. I should have put one of the younger men in charge. Someone like Culp. They think differently today. Me, I think like the old days. Men on horses robbing a bank or train, I can think the way they do and I belonged in the west, fit right in. Everything was simple, clear cut but this is so complicated, so involved, like that book Jekyll and Hyde. Or those stories about the detective in London. That's the kind of man who should be running an office in a city like this. He smiled to himself. Jesse James I could understand. In this kind of situation I'm lost but someone like Culp might not be. I know something's wrong but I don't know what it is or what to do about it.

He crouched behind a chair in the corner, the only one in the room. He had been there for hours now and soon she would come, too. She always came here when she wanted to be alone. He knew that, just as he knew she would come here before the wedding. She was like that, always wanting to be alone before something important happened. They had changed her, those others who pretended to be her friends, but she was still like that.

Not in other ways, though. They had changed her so she was just like them. He felt the blade of the knife and smiled. No, just like they *had* been. Had been before he changed *them*.

He suddenly tensed. Had that been a footstep on the stairs? There was only silence so little by little he relaxed. A mouse, probably, or the wind. But soon now she would be coming.

Why had they done it? Everything had been so perfect. Why couldn't they have left it that way? Why had they wanted to change it? They had been evil, that was why. And now she was just as bad. Worse, because they were gone now but still she was going ahead with it. Now it was too late. Nothing would ever be the same. Yes, she would be here soon. Here in her Secret Shrine. Then he would show her what she had done, what she had let happen. She would understand, then, but it would be too late. There was only one thing left to do now.

He tensed again. Then he smiled. There was no mistake this time. Footsteps on the stairs.

Cullan started when the telephone rang. The operative at the telegraph office, he thought, and picked up the receiver.

But it was a woman's voice and as he listened the color drained from his face. Then he shouted, "For God's sake, find her!" He dropped the receiver on the desk and jumped up. "Come on Culp! Marcia Telfare's disappeared!"

Culp waved toward Maynard. "What about him?"

" Forget him. Come on, hurry!"

Maynard had leaped up, too. "Marcia?" he said and then ran after them. "Wait, I'm going with you."

"What happened?" asked Culp when they were seated in a hansom cab speeding north on State Street.

Cullan was livid. "How could she slip away? All those people and less than an hour until the wedding. But she has. She was dressed and ready early and then just disappeared."

Maynard leaned forward in his seat. "At the Telfare house?"

Cullan nodded his head.

"Then I know where she is. The tower. The door to it opens off her bedroom but that end of the room has been sealed off to make a large closet. Only the family and a few old servants would know it's there and maybe they've forgotten about it." He sat back again. "She calls it her Secret Shrine."

Now Cullan bent forward. "And someone who knew her well would know she'd go there before the ceremony?"

Maynard nodded. "Anyone who really knew her would be certain of it."

Cullan leaned from the window and cried, "Faster, for God's sake," to the driver. When they at last arrived the three of them ran to the house. Cullan pushed people aside and told Maynard to lead the way. When they reached the closet it was Maynard and a long rack of clothes that he shoved from his path.

He found the door, jerked it open and raced up the stairs. At the top he stopped abruptly.

Marcus Telfare stood crouched over the chair in which his sister was slumped. The blade of the knife in his hand shone from the light of a single candle. The eyes he turned on Cullan glowed, too.

Cullan advanced slowly, his right hand extended. "Give it to me," he said quietly.

The youth straightened, turning at the same time. Cullan stopped and for a moment they stood that way, statues poised and unmoving. Then Marcus Telfare eased back and took a step up onto a window seat, still brandishing the knife.

To Cullan it was like a vivid tableau created by some mad artist. The youth poised on the ledge. Beyond him the brightly-lighted buildings downtown. Off to the left the lights of a ship on Lake Michigan and their reflection in the water.

He began slowly advancing again. Softly he repeated, "Give me the knife."

Fear suddenly welled up in the sick eyes in front of him. Marcus began shaking his head back and forth. "No," he cried and then again, softly, "No." He glanced quickly over his shoulder and then back again. Too late Cullan realized what he was going to do. He leaped but Marcus Telfare whirled and plunged through the glass.

Cullan walked to the shattered window and stood looking down. A moment or so passed and then he turned slowly back to Culp, "Better go down. No hurry. Don't say anything, leave that to me."

Maynard was kneeling in front of Marcia Telfare. She sat staring beyond him, transfixed, for several minutes. Then she focused her eyes on him and whispered, "Marcus. It was Marcus. Why? I don't understand."

Maynard took her hand. "He always had some sort of fixation. From the time we were children and he was only four or five. Didn't you know? Couldn't you see it?"

She shook her head.

"We used to joke about it, the rest of us. He idolized you. You were some sort of goddess to him. No one took it seriously, we thought it was just some boyhood thing he'd outgrow." Maynard shook his head, too. "My God, he must never have. Then, when you were going to get married, going to leave here — "

She began trembling, racked by unheard sobs. She leaned her head forward on Maynard's shoulder and put her arms around him. "Thank God you've come back," she whispered. He held her as Cullan watched silently for a moment and then walked quietly to the stairs. When he reached the main staircase he found a crowd huddled at its foot, held back by agency operatives. He descended slowly, looking around for the elder Telfare. When he saw him he said, "I have to talk to you and Mrs. Telfare in private."

He was following them toward a door when Teddy Winfield took hold of his arm. The young man's face was even more frigid than usual. Irritation smouldered in his eyes. "The wedding —" he began.

Cullan jerked his arm free. "It's off," he said and walked on.

ROCKY AND THE PHANTOM LADY

Gloria sways to the music, eyes closed, lips parted a little, fingers tapping out the beat on the tabletop. She drifts into the same trance-like state each time the song plays on the jukebox. She has claimed it as her own because the name of the song, like hers, is *Gloria*.

The back door of Horner's opens, then closes with a bang. Gloria jerks back to reality, turning to frown at the person responsible. It is Rocky Myers, a Midland detective and a regular on her annual list of the city's ten most detestable men. Rocky is fat, pompous, bald, and he smokes cigars. And if that were not enough to insure a place on Gloria's list, lechery gleams in his eyes whenever they fall upon her.

He sags down beside her in a chair that creaks under the strain, caresses her arm with dirty-nailed fingers, exhales the smoke from a fat corona in her face. Leaning closer, he croons, "Hi-yuh, sweet stuff."

She draws away from him, grimacing, and he laughs in the mistaken belief she is just pretending. Then, as an afterthought, he looks across the table at me and says, 'Hi-yuh, Blinn."

159

I nod in his direction, then look at Gloria. She has started to gather her things together, preparing to make a break for the door. I wink at her and smile. Then, as she pushes her chair back, she hesitates. Rocky has picked up the paperback in front of me and is studying the cover, scowling. His eyes rise slowly, settling on my face. "How come you happen to be reading this?"

"Why not?"

"This particular book, how come you happen to be reading it?"

"Why not?" I repeat, not comprehending his suspicious interest, but not really caring, either.

The impasse irritates Gloria. She turns to Rocky, saying, "Hal's reading it because I loaned it to him. What difference does it make?"

He settles back in his chair again, the scowl fading. "Just curious, little girl."

The pet names, which she considers derogatory, are just one more thing Gloria dislikes about him. She swings her chair around so she is farther away but facing him, black curls bouncing as she does so and a steely look in her eyes. "What do you know about that book?" she asks him.

"Nothing," he replies. "I remember it, that's all. And those mysteries, they're all alike – farfetched."

Keep it up, Rocky, I think to myself. Gloria loves mysteries.

"You've read *Phantom Lady*?" she asks disbelievingly.

"No, I never read that kinda stuff. Nothing like that ever happens in real life."

Gloria laughs deprecatingly. "You're a detective and you've never run across a mystery? Then what purpose do you serve? Why are the taxpayers paying you a salary?"

"Now back off," Rocky says, raising his hand. "I never said there wasn't crime. I meant it doesn't happen you have a guy murdered in a room with all the doors and windows locked from the inside. You know what I mean, where the guy leaves a clue, then some wiseacre comes along and figures it out. Stuff like that, it never happens."

I agree with him up to a point and almost sympathize because Gloria is aroused and will hang on like a bulldog. "So where does this particular book fit in?" I ask him.

He looks around, hoping he has found an ally. "It reminded me of something. Come to think of it, it proves my point."

Gloria leans closer to him, jaw set and fingers clenched. "I'll just bet it does. *Phantom Lady* happens to be a classic suspense story so naturally it proves there's no such thing as a real mystery. That makes a lot of sense."

"Tell us about it, Rock," I say, and Gloria mimics me, "Yes, by all means tell us about it, Rock."

He shifts his bulk uncomfortably. "Well, it was right after I made detective years ago. There was this case where I had the crazy idea maybe a guy had left a clue." He nods toward the book on the table. "And that was it."

"*Phantom Lady?*" Gloria and I say in unison.

"Yeah, *Phantom Lady*. See there was a burglar and this guy comes home and catches him in the act and gets a knife between the ribs. This was in the bedroom, and the guy wanders out to the living room and dies. As he's going down he takes the book with him, and me, being a dumb rookie, think maybe it's some kinda clue. You wouldn't believe the time I wasted checking it out."

Gloria's expression of outrage has been replaced by one of inquisitiveness. She leans even closer and asks, "What do you mean he took the book with him?"

"He staggered up against a bookcase and hung on for support. Then when he went down he took the book along."

"What exactly happened when the victim walked in on the intruder?" Gloria asks.

Rocky has begun to enjoy his new role. Before answering her he shakes a finger at me and says, 'Now none of this is gonna show up in that 'Around Town with Hal Blinn' column, understood?"

"Come off it, Rocky," I tell him. "If it's good, I use it. You know that."

"Then forget it," he says, shaking his head.

I start to reply but Gloria says, "Oh be quiet, Hal." Then to Rocky, "Go ahead, he won't use it in his column."

"Now wait a minute –" I begin, then shrug and mumble something under my breath. Suddenly I am the bad guy.

"Okay," Rocky says, pleased with himself. He lapses into police jargon, or something approaching a parody of it. "The subject arrives home from a VFW meeting, which he left early after becoming ill, and catches the perpetrator in the act. This was in the bedroom, where the subject's wife is asleep, also being sick and doped up on drugs."

"How do you know this if she was asleep?" I ask. Rocky gives me a pitying look. "Because that's where they fought and where the trail of blood began."

Makes sense, I think, but keep the thought to myself. "Go on," Gloria urges, annoyed by the interruption.

"Well, that was about it. The subject goes out in the living room and dies and the perpetrator takes off. Probably some punk on his first job and it scares hell out of him so it's his last job, too. All he had time to do was pull open a few drawers before the subject walked in on him."

"And the wife slept through it all?" I ask a little skeptically.

"Like I said, she was doped up."

"Funny the man didn't go to her for help after he was stabbed."

"And that was all?" asks Gloria, sounding deflated.

"Except for the time I wasted on that book idea," Rocky replies. He picks it up again, his scowl returning. "Hey, this isn't the right book. The one I'm talking about, it *was* written by a guy named William Irish. I won't forget that one in a hurry. I checked out every Mick in town thinking it might mean something. But this book, it was written by somebody named Cornell Woolrich."

"You should have checked further," I tell him. "Look at the fine print, Rocky. William Irish was a pseudonym. This is a reprint under his real name. Maybe someone who went to Cornell was the killer."

"Very funny," he says.

"Did you mean it about checking everything out?" asks Gloria.

"You bet I meant it. First the Irish angle, then every Bill he knew. Then the ladies in his life, only there weren't any phantom ladies hiding in that guy's closet."

"You should have read the book," Gloria says. "Then you would have known the killer's identity."

Rocky stares at her a moment, then puts his head back and laughs. I don't laugh, but I stare. Finally Rocky says, "Okay, chicky, wha'd'ya mean?"

"It really was a clue. The man didn't walk in on a burglar, he arrived home earlier than expected and found his wife in bed with his best friend. There was a fight and the friend killed him. The wife took the sleeping pills, or whatever they were, as a cover-up after he left."

Following a long silence Rocky says, "That's crazy. For one thing, the best friend was a guy I knew myself by the name of Ted Powell. The straightest arrow you ever saw and the Rock of Gibraltar after it happened. Why if it wasn't for him Marie – that's the wife - likely woulda gone off the deep end. As a matter of fact, about a year after it happened the two of them –" As his voice fades, a thoughtful look comes over Rocky's face.

"They did what?" asks Gloria. "Got married?"

"How'd you know?" Rocky asks suspiciously. "Are you familiar with this case?"

"How could I be? I've only been covering the school beat for the News-Banner the past four years. Before that I never heard of Midland." For a moment she sits smugly, then adds, "And I never heard of the people involved. I still don't know the victim's name."

Rocky sits quietly, mulling it over. He actually seems to take her wild guess seriously. Even I wonder about it, she seems so sure of herself. After a lengthy silence I say, "Gloria, where did you come up with that idea?"

She shakes her head. "I don't want to spoil the end of the story for you." Looking at Rocky again she says, "you going to follow up on it?"

"No way to. They're both dead, killed in a wreck somewhere out west a couple of years later."

"You really are taking this seriously, aren't you Rocky?" I ask him.

He hesitates, then says, "Naw. Anybody coulda come up with a guess like that."

"It wasn't a guess," Gloria says. "If you had read the book you'd have known it's the story of" – she pauses, looking across the table at me again – "I won't spoil it for you, Hal, but it's the story of a man betrayed by his best friend."

Rocky gets up suddenly, murmuring, "I gotta go." He drops a dollar on the table, then heads for the back door.

Gloria and I sit in silence for a moment or so before our eyes meet. She smiles, both dimples showing, but I just go on staring at her. When she picks her things up again I say, "You were putting him on, right?"

She lays her purse and notebooks back on the table. "I don't know. At first a little, maybe, because he made me mad. But after what he said about them –"

She settles back in her chair, thinking. I signal for two more drinks, then pick up a quarter and walk over to the jukebox.

This time she forgets to go into her trance when the first notes of *Gloria* fill the room. She goes on staring at the table for a while, then looks up suddenly. She is smiling again, this time pensively. "I was right, Hal. I'm sure I was, and so was Rocky."

"Come on, Gloria, things don't happen that way in real life." I pick up the book and study the picture of a woman standing under a light on a deserted subway platform. In the foreground the shadow of an approaching man is barely visible. I turn to the title page, then one more, and read a quote by someone named John Ingall – "I answer not and I return no more."

I wonder.

BEANBALL

Some said there was bad blood between them, others contended Mangrum's high hard one just got away from him. I kept my mouth shut, but I can verify that in the open press box at Three Rivers Stadium you could hear bone splintering when the ball met Tommy Hartsfield's cheek at just under one hundred miles an hour.

Turk Macy was out of the Stars' dugout, charging the mound with mayhem in mind even before Hartsfield began writhing in the dirt of the batter's box. Lee Mangrum retreated toward center field but Macy was cut off at the baseline by Tucker Nolan, the coach at first base.

That was all the action. Ten minutes passed before the people working over Hartsfield straightened up and attendants lifted him to an ambulance. Then Jack Lane, the Stars' publicity director, picked up the phone to the dugout. He listened quietly for a moment, then passed the word that Hartsfield's cheekbone was shattered but as far as those on the field could tell the eye wasn't damaged.

Long before that I got up and walked to the refreshment area, shaky inside and thinking to hell with my pledge to lay off the beer until the work was finished and my story filed. I wouldn't have wanted such a thing to happen to anyone, least of all a gentle person like Tommy Hartsfield. Losing their second baseman in mid-August could kill the Stars' hope of a pennant, too, but at the moment I didn't care.

My despondency persisted through the afternoon, even when the Stars staved off a ninth-inning Pittsburgh uprising and won 5-4. I jotted down a few clubhouse quotes, trite as usual and loaded with clichés, then took a cab to the hotel to write the story in the seclusion of my room.

A few people, none of them connected with the ball club, were in the lobby of the William Penn when I settled in a chair about seven and ordered a tall vodka and soda. I like the lobby better than any around the league but for once the luxurious surroundings failed to relax me or relieve the queasy feeling in my stomach. Freddy DeAngelo walked by looking as if he carried the cares of the world on his shoulders. Freddy inherited second base when Hartsfield was injured. Now the pressure of carrying the load during the stretch drive would be on the little utility infielder, and I sympathized. Turk Macy went by, too, grim-faced as he headed for the street. He and Hartsfield had been roommates for three years.

I was considering a second drink when Pat McGann, the Stars' manager, hurried by toward the door, then stopped when he saw me and walked over to my table. McGann said, "I got two tickets to the Wayne Newton show, wanna come along? Tuck Nolan was goin' but he's outta the mood. Myself, I could do with somethin' to take my mind off things."

I wasn't in the mood, either, although it had seemed Newton was following our road trip from city to city and I had been wanting to catch his act. But I needed column material and being alone with a manager always offers the possibility of learning something of interest to the readers back home. Under the circumstances that would be speculation by McGann as to how Hartsfield's absence would affect the Stars' chances for a pennant. I got up, reluctantly though, and fell in step beside McGann.

The show was at Heinz Hall, a civic center dating back to the 1920s when Loew's was building ornate theaters in cities around the country. Pittsburgh got a miniature of the palace at Versailles – marble columns, gold leaf, red velvet. At one side was a lounge and beyond it an open courtyard with tables. When the show ended I bought drinks and led McGann to a table near a fake waterfall.

166

"Good show," I said mechanically. Then, after a lengthy silence, "Think DeAngelo can handle second base?"

McGann stared into the cascading water. "I dunno. Maybe. For insurance we put in a call to Louisville. The Egan kid's flyin' in in the morning."

"Bobby Egan? He hasn't been hitting, has he?"

"Not at first he wasn't. Not after we sent him down in the spring, but he's picked up a little lately. Some people don't hit as good in Triple-A as they do here. You know – better lights, better pitchin' so you can dig a toehold."

Sure, I thought, like Tommy Hartsfield. But Egan's background and prospects were the start of a column and I was able to pry a few more bits of information from McGann during the walk back to the hotel.

As we approached the door Joe Tyner, the club's traveling secretary, charged out, wild-eyed. He pulled up short when he saw McGann, relief draining the tension from his face. "God, I'm glad you're back," he said. "Turk Macy's in jail. I'm on my way down to get him out."

"Jail?" said McGann. "Wha'd'ya mean, jail? For what?"

Tyner turned back to him after motioning the doorman to hold the only cab at the stand. "Assault. I guess he caught up with Lee Mangrum and damn near killed him."

I started to crowd in the cab behind them, then changed my mind and went inside the William Penn to the nearest phone. After verifying the charge, then learning from Jack Lane that Mangrum was in a coma, I called the newspaper and dictated a brief for page one.

Tyner and McGann arranged bail for Macy and the three of them returned to the hotel about one in the morning. It wasn't until breakfast, though, that I had an opportunity to talk to Turk. By then the anger that was evident when he arrived from jail had given way to depression.

Macy denied having any part in the beating. "How long you known me?" he asked. "Did I ever lie to you? Name one time, just one. Hell, I never beat up Mangrum – it was me that run off the two guys who were workin' him over."

I bit into a roll, studying the stocky outfielder. "Okay, so what did happen?"

"I went over there mad, sure. Up on Mount Washington where I knew Mangrum had an apartment. I figured he'd be out boozing and he was, in a little bar down the street from where you get off the incline. We had a few things to say to each other and maybe I would've done more'n talk but a couple of his cronies grabbed me about then and Mangrum left. So did I, two maybe three minutes later when his buddies let go. That's when I seen the two guys beating on Mangrum in the parking lot. Like I said, they took off when I showed up and then I could see Mangrum was hurt bad. The next thing you know there's a crowd around and everybody think's it was me that done it."

"Mangrum can tell them otherwise, can't he?" As soon as I said it I remembered the Pittsburgh pitcher was in a coma so I added, a little lamely, "Provided he comes to."

Macy grimaced, holding up the palms of both hands. "How do I know what he can tell 'em? He was out like a light by the time I got there."

I stood for a while by the batting cage with the other writers, watching dark storm clouds that didn't relieve the Sunday afternoon heat. The Stars' mood during batting practice was as forbidding as the skies. A rainout would be welcome, I decided. That, along with the open date on Monday, might allow time to regroup before the Tuesday flight to Philadelphia for a decisive series with the only team ahead of them in the standings.

The skies brightened, but for the Stars the afternoon continued bleak. In the bottom of the first inning what should have been a double-play ball to retire the side instead caromed off the glove of Freddy DeAngelo. That brought Madlock up with the bases loaded and he parked the second pitch in the bullpen beyond the fence. It ended 4-1, with the Stars' morale another notch down the scale.

After filing my story a little after five, I crossed the Monongahela by cab, then rode the century-old Duquesne Incline to the top of Mount Washington, Lee Mangrum's territory. From a window table at LeMont, a restaurant I enjoy for the food and the view of the city, the rivers, and the stadium, I watched absently as people began drifting away from a festival that was breaking up at the point where the Allegheny and Monongahela join to form the Ohio River. The feeling gnawed at me that I wasn't doing my job, that I was missing the real story. If Turk Macy had told the truth, and I believed he had, then the beating of Lee Mangrum was connected with his personal life and had nothing to do with Saturday's beanball pitch.

Mangrum was the flashy sort that comes along now and then; a kid with a blazing fastball but a playboy from the time he broke in with Los Angeles. He had a great rookie season until near its end, but then tapered off fast as the Hollywood lifestyle took its toll. After a couple of mediocre years the Dodgers unloaded him. For a while the change of scenery seemed to help but the word around the league was that Mangrum had gradually developed his own cult of swingers and spent a lot of time with unsavory characters.

When the remains of my dinner had been cleared away and my coffee cup was empty for the third time, I settled the bill, then walked aimlessly in the warm night air above the city. I passed the building where Mangrum lived, then the bar, closed now, where the beating had occurred. A waste of time, I decided, and headed back to the hotel. There Jack Lane told me Mangrum had regained consciousness but claimed he had been attacked from behind and didn't see a thing. Turk Macy remained on the bubble.

I was on the street early Monday morning. It's my favorite time of day in any city – that brief interlude when the air is fresh, people haven't started arriving for work, yet you can sense the coming activity. A cab took me across the Monongahela again, but this time down Carson Street to a workers' neighborhood near the Jones and Laughlin mills. It was an old but busy part of town, rich in ethnic flavor, the place where Al Koloski operated a newsstand close to the intersection of two narrow, crowded streets.

Koloski, at sixty still a man with powerful shoulders and biceps that rippled under his sleeves, was stacking newspapers just inside the door. An ex-ballplayer and an ex-con, he had never forgotten a story I had written a dozen years earlier

169

contending his prison record shouldn't keep him out of the Hall of Fame at Cooperstown. The story didn't accomplish anything but no one else had ever bothered to express the thought. From that day on I could do no wrong in the eyes of Al Koloski.

"So what brings you around?" he said. "Too bad about Tommy Hartsfield, but that isn't it. The Macy-Mangrum business, right?"

"You called it, Al. What can you tell me?"

"Not much, but it only happened Saturday night so I haven't seen many people. I can tell you this, Mangrum ran with a bad crowd and there's a lot the ball club and the commissioner's office don't know about. Not yet, anyway."

"Such as?"

"Such as Mangrum being into high-stake gambling. He's been laying some heavy bets, sometimes on ball games. And if that isn't enough to finish him when the word gets to the right places, they say he's supporting his betting habit by peddling the hard stuff to his crowd."

"Sounds like he's a busy boy. Who can I talk to?"

"You might check out Frankie Martin's gambling operation. But carefully, friend – you know how Frankie operates. As for drugs, a guy they call Jackley, he's your man. Chances are you'll catch him in the taproom around the corner this time of day. A skinny, weasel-faced guy in a white suit, winter or summer. I hear he's Mangrum's source."

The workingman's tavern was crowded for early morning but with Koloski's description guiding me it was easy to pick out Jackley standing at the far end of the bar. He wasn't a friendly man, or a talkative one, but a little power-of-the-press persuasion oiled his tongue enough to tell me all I wanted to know. Mangrum was buying all right, and a lot more than needed for a one-man habit.

After walking around a couple of blocks to be sure I hadn't sprouted a tail, I headed for a nearby restaurant. It's a large, plush layout where top dollar buys you good food, strong drink, and live entertainment six nights a week. A moneymaker, yet only a front for Frankie Martin's gambling network that brings in the really big bucks.

170

I got to know the basics of the operation a few years earlier when Martin made one of his infrequent appearances in court. An outfielder on the Stars, a big name, was involved so I covered what little there was to cover. The player had tried to clear himself by dragging Martin into the mess. Some of what he said was true but most was pure fabrication so the case against Martin was dropped after the preliminaries. Before that happened I learned how the tentacles of Martin's operation reached into every factory in his territory, raking in thousands daily from workers playing the numbers and the horses.

Not much of that showed up in my stories because knowing it and proving it are two different things, either in court or in print. I did my best to write objectively about everyone involved, which wasn't always easy. I guess Frankie Martin felt I succeeded because he approached me the next time the Stars were in Pittsburgh and said, "Some of that stuff you wrote, I wish you hadn't. But what you wrote, it was accurate, which is more'n I can say for most of what I read. What I mean is, you didn't color it up and I appreciate that."

We talked briefly, then I talked and Frankie listened quietly. When I finished he said, "The only thing surprises me, you oughta know better'n to think I'd get tied up with a ball player. C'mon now, those guys are dynamite. Sure, I hear Mangrum lays some heavy bets, but either outta town or with private parties. Nobody local'd touch him. Pros, I mean. Me, I wouldn't even let that punk eat'n my place."

"You make it sound personal."

He nodded once, making it emphatic, then walked to the door of his apartment and said, "C'mon." I followed him along a hallway past closed doors, then down a half-flight of stairs to a sundeck overlooking a landscaped courtyard. A girl in her early twenties sat in a wheelchair, empty faced, looking out but seeing nothing. A light robe over her legs didn't hide the fact they were too thin, too misshapen. A nurse or companion looked up briefly, then returned to her book.

Martin laid his hand on the girl's shoulder without speaking, then turned and led me back the way we had come. When we were in his office again he lit a cigarette. "My daughter, the only one. A bright young kid, a junior at Pitt before the accident. I'm just glad my wife didn't live to see it."

I waited, knowing he intended to tell me what happened and having a pretty good idea what it would be.

After a few seconds he said, "A party. Booze, then drugs on toppa that. Got halfway home in one of those little foreign convertible jobs, they met a semi on a hill."

"This party, it was at Lee Mangrum's?"

He nodded, just barely. "So I guess you could say I had a reason to want to see Mangrum hurt. But if it had been me, he wouldn't be in any hospital."

I believed that, but it put me back at the plate with two strikes against me. Martin studied me a moment, then said, "Your interest, it's clearing Turk Macy, right?"

"That, and doing my job. So where do I go, any ideas?"

"Back to the hotel. Gimme three hours'n I'll call you."

There weren't many options open, so that's what I did. Martin called fifteen minutes ahead of time. "The party I think you might be interested in, his name's Brad McPhee. An account executive at an advertising agency downtown. Has a pretty young wife, but they say she hasn't been spending much time at home lately."

"What happened to Mangrum," I said a little skeptically, "it doesn't sound like the work of an advertising man."

"It wasn't, not personally. The strong arms belong to a pair of freelancers, Pete Vaccaro and Nappy LaRue. They hang out in a bar downstairs where McPhee's office is, The Lilac Tree. Pete and Nappy hire out for anything you can name, but they don't work cheap and they don't leave calling cards behind. As I see it, all you can do's talk to the people handling Macy's case, without mentioning where you heard it, and hope they check it out and drop whatever they're charging Macy with. Of course they may get around to that without you horning in."

They might, but it could take time and the plane for Philadelphia would leave the next morning. It took a while to get to the right people, and when I did the two detectives, Klein and Benevides, weren't thrilled to have a newspaperman, especially one from out of town, passing along tips. I didn't blame them, I'd feel the same way about cops telling me how to write a story. It ended with them telling me they'd check it out and me feeling they were already doing it before I got there. When you get right down to it, their sources and Frankie Martin's wouldn't be all that different.

When I got back to the William Penn I was feeling pretty good. Turk Macy would be cleared, I felt sure of it, and when he was I'd have background information that would enable me to write the best story in either the Pittsburgh papers or those back home.

Then I made my big mistake. I told Turk Macy. When looking back on it, it seems like the right thing to have done because it should have relieved his mind a little. What it did, though, was make him explode.

He squirmed around, barely able to stay in his chair until I finished talking. Then he leaped up, shouting, "I'm goin' down to that bar and look those babies up."

"Now hold on, Turk, you can't do that. You'll spoil everything."

"I can't, huh? Now don't gemme wrong, I appreciate what you done, but don't tell me I can't go down there."

I said, "Turk, you can't go down –" but then stopped because the door had already closed behind him. I grabbed the phone, dialed Jack Lane's room, told him to call Klein and Benevides, then headed for The Lilac Tree on the double.

It was the beginning of happy hour. In fact the fun was well under way by the time I arrived because few newspapermen can keep pace with a leftfielder, especially one with a head start. I'm not sure what happened before I got there, but obviously Turk had found his men and had not bothered with a diplomatic approach. The crowd had separated like fans when a line foul screams into the stands. Turk, struggling mightily but in vain, was being escorted through the opening, each arm in the vise-like grip of a very big, very muscular man. The Brooks Brothers suits they wore did nothing to conceal their line of work.

I did the only thing I could think of, stepped in front of them and said, "Now hold on a minute." Then I repeated it because the man nearest me had slipped his free hand under my arm and I was part of the group headed for a door at the rear of the lounge.

Just where we were going I wasn't sure, although I could have taken an educated guess. But before we got to the door it opened and Benevides stood there, grinning wickedly. "Well, Pete and Nappy," he said. "Going somewhere boys?"

Pete and Nappy, being no fools, decided they weren't.

Turk walked back to where I was sitting, settled in the seat beside me, then sat without saying anything as we cruised 25,000 feet above the Pennsylvania hills. He wanted to say thanks but wasn't sure how to begin.

The charge against him had been dismissed. Klein and Benevides had been doubtful about getting anything to stick against Pete Vaccaro and Nappy LaRue until Lee Mangrum suddenly panicked and began acting less like a Pirate than a cardinal in spring. He had recognized them, he said, then went on to tell everything he knew about Jackley and a number of other citizens of Pittsburgh and half a dozen different cities around the league. It wouldn't do him any good, his career in baseball was finished.

Tommy Hartsfield would be out of the hospital in a week. By then the Stars would be starting a long homestand but Tommy would spend what was left of the season in Pine Bluff, Arkansas. He would be missed, of course, but the events of Monday afternoon had acted like a tonic on the rest of the players. Their poise had returned, and their confidence. The flight to Philadelphia took only an hour, but they couldn't wait to get there.

We came in low over Veterans Stadium and somebody yelled, "Hey, there's The Vet down there. Look, one of the Phillies is out taking extra batting practice."

Turk laughed. "He's smart. They're gonna need all the help they can get."

I grinned. Things were back to normal.

WHAT WOULD YOU HAVE DONE?

Everyone in the village must be shocked by what happened in the house out back. Shocked but probably not surprised. That's a surmise on my part because I've missed all the excitement lying here in bed with two broken legs.

Justin, my boy, tells me the diner's been closed the last few days while the out-of-town owner tries to find someone to run it. That's what brought the Rolfe family here six years ago. Ted, the father, took over as manager. He and Jenny, his wife, and their eleven-year-old son Ralph needed a place to live, so I rented them the old house at the back of my property.

Before Ted arrived the only people who patronized the diner were strangers who didn't know better. The food was terrible and the manager and only waitress tried to outdo each other in being nasty.

Ted changed that in a hurry. He got rid of the waitress and hired a couple of girls who knew how to smile. He was a first-rate cook and had the knack of making people feel at home. It didn't take him long to learn the names of everyone in this part of the county. He kept up a steady banter with the customers and within a month the diner was the most popular place in town.

Jenny Rolfe was as well liked as her husband. She was a small, almost frail woman with a warm smile and a real affinity for people. For the first five years Jenny spent a lot of time at the diner, helping serve when the place was busy or taking the money at the register. Most of the time, though, she would just visit with the customers. She would sit down and they'd talk back and forth and before long it seemed like Ted and Jenny Rolfe had been around town all their lives.

Ralph was something else again. I sized him up as a rat the minute I laid eyes on him and nothing ever happened to change my mind. But a family of rodents wouldn't have put up with him. It wasn't long before it was a popular topic around here; how could two people as nice as Ted and Jenny have a mean, rotten kid like that? I sure didn't know the answer.

What bothered me right from the start was that Ralph had things all his own way. I don't think either Ted or Jenny ever took a belt to him and God knows he needed it. Even when he was only eleven some of the things he said to his parents were so bad I never repeated them because no one would have believed me. He didn't improve with age.

That first spring they were here Jenny planted rows of flowers along each side of the driveway back by their house. I wasn't around much but usually when I'd stop by she'd be working on them, really enjoying herself. Had a talent for it, too, a regular green thumb.

I happened to be home the day Ralph rode his bicycle over both rows. By the time he'd had his fun there wasn't a thing standing an inch above the ground. I looked out the window when I heard Jenny say, "Oh, Ralph, why?"

He had a sneer on his face. For a few seconds he laughed at her. Then he said, "I'm hungry. Fix me somethin' to eat."

Jenny had a stricken look and it seemed to me that when she turned from the trampled flowers to her son she was wondering what kind of monster she had brought into the world. But she went inside and a few minutes later called, "Your lunch is ready, son."

One flower had popped back up a little. Ralph finished grinding it into the dirt with his heel and then sat down with his back against a tree. "Bring it out here," he yelled. She brought it out to him on a tray.

Jenny never planted flowers again but that was just one of a hundred or more incidents I witnessed even though I wasn't around the place too often. The worst that ever resulted was Ted or Jenny would say, "Ralph, I wish you hadn't done that," or, "You shouldn't talk that way, son." His response was always predictable.

From the stories I heard, Ralph was just as bad at school and around the village. The classic bully, only meaner than most. A kid who loved to destroy or deface anything people valued. The older he got, the more damage he did.

Probably the only real beating he ever took came from me. I was in the living room one day when Ralph was about fifteen. Without warning there was a shotgun blast right outside. He had killed a rabbit not ten feet from my front door.

He stood there sneering at me until I leaped at him from the front porch. After a minute or two he was pleading for mercy. When I cooled down a little, I let him up but not before I took the shell out of the second barrel. Then I stood over him while he repaired the damage the shot had done to the porch railing. It was the last time I ever saw him with the shotgun and believe me, with a punk like that I kept an eye out for it.

The accident happened a few weeks ago on the highway between my place and the village. A drunk swerved at the last second and hit me head on. The seat went forward and snapped both my legs. After a few days in the hospital Justin brought me home when I refused to go to his place. He stops over every morning and cleans up and brings along a combination breakfast and lunch. Then he comes by again about two-thirty in the afternoon on his way to work the three o'clock shift at the wire mill. He leaves a cold supper for me and stops on his way home a little after eleven so I get by all right.

It's funny the things you learn when you're flat on your back and people gradually forget you're around. The thing that really stunned me was finding out that Ted Rolfe was a wife beater. He was the last man on earth I would have pegged as one.

Ted would usually come home about two o'clock in the afternoon. By then the lunch hour rush at the diner was over and he'd stay a couple of hours before heading back to handle the supper trade. I had noticed that Jenny seldom went to the diner the past year so maybe the beatings were a recent development. He'd slap her around pretty good though. Enough so I could hear it thirty yards away. Then sometimes I'd hear Jenny outside crying a little. A few months ago her face was all bruised up. She told me she had fallen down and at the time I had no reason to doubt her.

Of course Ralph was as miserable as ever. A week ago he was loafing around when his mother called, "Ralph, your dad wants you to help him carry out the trash."

It was quiet for a few seconds and then his mother called, "Ralph," again. This time the kid answered. "Tell the old bastard to do it himself."

I lay there cursing under my breath, wishing I could get up and thrash him myself. Jenny had come closer and I could hear her say kind of softly, "Oh, Ralph, I wish you wouldn't say things like that." He laughed at her.

Three days ago Ted came home about two o'clock as usual. Half an hour later Justin stopped by with my supper. He stayed and talked for fifteen minutes and then left for the wire mill.

He had been gone maybe ten minutes when Ted started giving Jenny a bad time again. He ranted and raved a couple of minutes and then I heard flesh strike flesh. By then I was sick of it so I used the remote control to switch on the TV and watched a soap opera where the people *really* had problems.

It was about ten after three when I heard the shotgun blast. I flipped off the TV and listened but there wasn't another sound. I thought about calling the sheriff but when it had been quiet for five minutes or so I figured they were talking rationally for a change and decided there was no point in embarrassing them. It might just make it worse for Jenny.

The bus from the high school dropped Ralph off about quarter to four. I heard him shuffle along the driveway and knew the peace and quiet at the house out back was about to be shattered. I was right. Ralph just about had time to get there when the shotgun blasted away again.

Of course by then I knew something was badly wrong. I suppose I should have called the sheriff and I still can't really say why I didn't.

There wasn't another sound from out back and it stayed that way for three hours. Then the screen door slammed and the car started. I reached over and switched on my lamp but there was a brilliant flash and then semi-darkness again. The bulb had burned out. I lay there in the dusk and waited for the car to pull out of the driveway. It never did. For twenty minutes the motor idled, then it was shut off and I heard the door slam again.

Another ten minutes passed and it was totally dark by then. A car turned in at the drive and when it passed my window I could see a red globe on top and knew it was a sheriff's cruiser.

The minutes dragged while I lay there listening to the sounds out back: doors slamming, footsteps, the crackling of the police radio. Voices, too, but too soft to hear what they were saying. Then a couple more vehicles pulled in the driveway. There was a lot of activity but I had no way of knowing what was going on.

When things started to settle down I heard footsteps on the porch and then Bill Tompkins, the sheriff, called, "Anybody home?"

I yelled, "Come on in, Bill, and turn on some lights." He did, out in the living room, and then I told him where the spare bulbs were and he replaced the one in my lamp.

He pulled a chair up close to the bed and sat stroking his chin for a minute. Finally he said, "Know what happened out back?"

I shook my head.

"Ted Rolfe killed his son with a shotgun and then used the second barrel on himself."

I gave a low whistle. The sheriff said, "Didn't you hear the shots?"

I nodded.

"Didn't you wonder about them?"

"You hear shots out here in the country now and then, even out of hunting season. How'd you find out about it?"

"Jenny called. She'd been down in Indianapolis since the middle of the afternoon. Got back half an hour ago and found them. God, what a shock that must have been for her."

"Is she okay?"

"She's still in shock, I think. It hasn't really soaked in yet."

"You say she was in Indianapolis?"

The sheriff nodded. "Yeah. She must have called as soon as she got back because the hood of the car was still warm. She said she left when Ted came home from the diner after lunch. I asked her how he was going to get back and she told me he was going to walk since it was a nice day. It's better'n a mile but she says he liked to do that and I guess I do remember seeing him walking it sometimes."

"It's not a bad walk when the weather's nice. Do it myself once in awhile."

"Did you hear the car?"

I nodded again. "Yeah, I heard it."

The sheriff sighed and stood up. "It's a messy business but I guess that wraps it up. It's good that you heard the shots and the car. That kind of verifies everything."

"Right. I heard the shots and the car."

Bill left and the activity outside went on a while longer, but since then it's been quiet out back. Justin tells me that Jenny stayed at the motel on the other side of the village until after the funerals this morning. Then she left and I'm sure she won't be back.

It's strange, that light bulb burning out when it did so the house stayed dark. Things might have worked out differently otherwise. Maybe not, of course.

One thing I learned is that a person can tell the truth and not tell the truth at the same time if the questions are worded right and there aren't too many of them.

I was afraid I'd have visitors nosing around but so far I've been lucky. By the time I'm back on my feet the excitement should have died away. Someday I'll be asked about that afternoon, I know, and the questions may be put differently than when the sheriff asked them. But I'll give the same answers I gave Bill Tompkins.

What would you have done?

A DOG'S BEST FRIEND

The oversized mongrel stood patiently while his master worked with shaky fingers on the knot that would secure the rope leash to a metal post. Satisfied, the old man stroked the dog's head and said, "Now you wait right here, Blackie. I won't be long and then we'll get you a nice treat."

Blackie settled himself on the warm concrete, forelegs crossed, chin resting on them, watery old eyes fixed on the pawnshop door his master had entered. The routine was familiar, but Blackie never felt comfortable until the old man reappeared.

Bennie Lowe watched from a doorway fifty feet away. He often had noticed the old man and his dog and now a plan took shape in Bennie's mind. Few people were on the street so it would be a piece of cake, he thought, a pushover.

A few minutes passed, Blackie watching the door, Bennie watching it too. When the old man came out patting the pocket of the shabby jacket containing his wallet, Bennie moved quickly. The old man had taken only a few steps when strong hands grabbed him from behind, one reaching for the opening of the jacket.

"Gimme that, man," Bennie snarled.

"No!" cried the old man, clamping his right arm over the front of the jacket, struggling to keep his assailant's hand from getting inside.

Blackie, teeth bared and growling deep in his throat, lunged toward them but the rope held.

The tussle continued a few seconds, Bennie gradually gaining the upper hand. When the wallet finally was in his grip he gave the old man a hard shove, then turned and ran toward a nearby alley. The old man staggered back, fighting to regain his balance. His wobbly legs failed him and he fell hard, striking his head on a jagged break between strips of concrete.

Still Blackie tried to reach him, but the rope held firm. A man ran from the pawnshop and knelt beside the old man. Others hurried up and the kneeling man told the first, "Call the police and an ambulance."

Blackie, confused, excited, paced back and forth, whimpering and trying every few seconds to get to his master.

Within moments a police car pulled to the curb near the crowd gathered around the still figure on the sidewalk. A young policeman herded the bystanders away while his middle-aged partner crouched beside the old man, feeling for a pulse. When the young policeman bent down the other stared at him, raising his eyebrows. "I think we got ourselves a murder, buddy," he said softly.

Blackie continued to pace and whine during the few minutes it took the ambulance to arrive. Two paramedics worked briefly over the old man, then lifted the frail body onto a stretcher. As they carried it to the ambulance Blackie howled mournfully, straining at his leash, still unable to reach his master.

"That's his dog," said one of the onlookers. The young policeman edged near Blackie, talking softly, trying to calm him. As the ambulance pulled away Blackie let out a frenzied howl and lunged after it. The rope still held but the worn leather collar snapped. Blackie raced down the street, continuing the chase long after the ambulance had disappeared in the distance.

Bennie Lowe read the newspaper story hesitatingly, sounding out the words with his lips and shaking his head.

"Crazy ol' man," he muttered to himself. "Why'd he go an' gimme trouble like this?"

He looked up and down the street warily, then aloud said, "I better split this place a while." The newspaper fell from his fingers as he walked quickly away in the direction of the bus station.

Joe Hanley let the report drop to the desk top and leaned back in his chair, eyes not seeing the smoky buff wall they had settled on. He poked a finger around in his right ear and said, "From the description we got, it could be about anybody."

His partner, Caproletti, waved his hand deprecatingly. "You call that a description? It's *nothing*. All we can do is wait and see what we get back from the street, if anything."

"Yeah, I know. I guess nobody's going to get too excited about it, anyway. No survivors, just a few cronies as old as he was. It burns me, though. An eighty-year-old man downtown in broad daylight and with a dog, even."

"What about the dog?"

"Hasn't turned up yet. Probably ran itself to death after that ambulance or got hit along the way."

The sign on the bank across from the park displayed 78 degrees but a heavy sweater and wool jacket hung loosely on the shoulders of the man who approached the bench with jerky, stiff-legged steps. He eased himself down beside the pair already there and said, "I seen Blackie again but he wouldn't come to me just like before. I can't figure what's wrong with him."

The man at the far end snorted. "He lost his best friend and he don't have a home, that's what's wrong with him."

"But what's he eating?" whined the first man. "And where's he staying nights?"

"He's eating outta the cans and he's probably spending his nights right here in the park."

"Too bad," said the man in the middle. "Old Jack'd feel bad if he knew about that."

"Well, I done everything I know how," the first man said. "Blackie just don't seem to want to have nothing to do with his old friends."

Jonas Decker stood scowling on the sidewalk outside his men's wear store. "There's that dog again," he called to the man washing a window thirty feet away. The man glanced over his shoulder to the other side of the street and nodded.

"I don't like it," Jonas continued. "It's not good for business, having a dog running around loose like that all the time. Scares off customers."

The other man leaned the long-handled squeegee against the window and walked over, grinning. "It's not the dog that scares off customers, Jonas, it's your prices. That dog's not doing any harm, he's just looking for his master. He won't give up and it's kind of sad after all this time."

"Sad, is it? Scary, I'd call it. Look at him sniffing at people like he always does. I don't care what you say, that dog's dangerous."

The other man chuckled. "I told you, Jonas, he's looking for his master."

"Can't he tell his master without sniffing at everybody? Besides, that old man's been dead three months so if that dog hasn't any better sense than to think he's coming back it just proves he shouldn't be hanging around like he does. I can't figure what's wrong with those people out at the animal shelter. I've called three times now and you'd think they could manage to catch one old dog."

His companion shook his head. "They'll never catch that dog, Jonas, so you might just as well accept the fact. Forget about it, that dog's not bothering you any."

"He'll bother somebody one of these days, mark my words. I've a good notion to bring a gun down here and get rid of it myself."

The other man laughed and turned back toward his store. "That dog's no more dangerous than I am, Jonas. But let me know if you bring that gun down because I don't want to be out on the street when some old fool starts shooting one off."

"Looks like we can put this one at the back of the drawer, Cap," said Hanley. He tapped the bottom of a file folder on the desk and studied his partner's response.

Caproletti nodded. "It could have been there all along, Joe. Unless we get a break when we collar somebody on another charge we can forget it."

"I hear the dog's been hanging around the low end of downtown."

"Still trying to find the old man, I guess."

"Think so, Cap? Maybe he's looking for the guy that killed him."

Caproletti grinned. "Sure, Joe. Now we've got dog detectives, huh? Well, I hope his luck is better'n ours."

Bennie Lowe glanced around cautiously as he stepped off the Trailways bus, then chided himself for being foolish. No one was looking for him; he was home scot-free. The police didn't have a thing to go on, not one. And they wouldn't get one, he thought, pleased with his cleverness in pulling the job without leaving a trace and then having the good sense to get out of town a while, just in case.

He walked three blocks east to Main Street, then south to the old neighborhood. His first stop, he decided, would be the liquor store for a bottle and then he'd check his old building, see if a room was available.

The dog came up on him from behind, sniffing at his pant leg. Bennie snarled, "Get away, mutt!" and lashed out at it with his foot.

"I knew it," exclaimed Jonas Decker. "I told them that dog was dangerous but nobody paid any attention. Now look what's happened."

"You see it?" asked Hanley.

"Yes I saw it. I've been watching that animal, I knew it was vicious. You know who's to blame for this, don't you? Those people at the animal shelter. All the times I called out there and they couldn't even catch one dog."

Hanley nodded toward the other side of the street where a man was muzzling the black dog lying quietly on the sidewalk in front of the pawnshop. "Doesn't look like the guy's having any trouble with him now."

"Sure, now that it's too late."

Hanley walked across to where Caproletti was standing and watched as the old dog was lifted into the caged bed of a pickup truck. "Good thing we came out, Cap. Decker says it's the old man's dog, all right."

He kneeled beside the body a moment, then looked up. "Doesn't look like he even bit the guy."

"He didn't," said Caproletti. "You know who it is, don't you? Our old friend Bennie Lowe."

Hanley straightened up, nodding. He gave Caproletti an owlish look. "Think maybe it worked out like we were talking about? That dog's been sniffing at people right along, but this is the first one he's gone after."

Caproletti flashed a sneer at his partner. "Come on, Joe, you know better. So it's the kind of job Bennie Lowe might have pulled, what's that prove? Bennie gives the dog a good kick, the dog snaps at him, Bennie runs, trips over that jagged break there in the concrete and smashes his head against the post. It's as simple as that."

Hanley grinned a little. "Maybe, Cap. Maybe it won't go in the report, but what you wanna bet we won't be pulling that file again?"

FATHER'S GIRL
Originally titled "Missing"

I watched the exchange from the corner of my eye. I wasn't interested, just a little amused. The two men in three-piece suits were so intent on being secretive they had attracted my attention.

No one else in the riverfront diner knew anything was going on. An old woman with matted hair and gnarled features hovered over a plate of donuts, fearful someone might snatch one away. At the far end of the counter a man wearing jeans and a dirty T-shirt was lost in the sports section of the Louisville Times' Indiana edition. The waitress, a teenager with too many pounds and a mottled complexion, was more interested in a phone conversation than her customers.

The first man was tall with rounded shoulders under a mane of unruly dark hair. A large brown envelope was under one arm when he came in. The second entered soon after, looked around and then sat down next to him on the empty half of a double stool. The brown envelope was between them. Neither spoke but anyone watching could tell they were aware of each other.

The second man was shorter, older, and heavier. After a few sips of coffee he took a business-size white envelope from the inside pocket of his jacket and laid it down beside the other. The tall man picked it up quickly, then dropped it. The second time he managed to tuck it away in his own pocket.

The short man drank more coffee, then got up and left. The brown envelope was in his right hand. It was an amateurish performance, but no one else had noticed. That's the way it is, people too wrapped up in themselves to see what's going on unless it's flashed in front of them on a television screen.

I followed the short man outside. He walked north on Spring Street past the floodwall to a burgundy Buick Riviera facing south. As he drove by I made a mental note of the license number, then took a final look at the choppy gray water and walked north myself.

When I got to the top of the stairs, Selma Olds greeted me with the smile she pastes on when someone is sharing her reception area. Then in the starchy tone reserved for formal occasions she said, "Mrs. Mannweiler is here to see you, Mr. Rakich."

If Mrs. Mannweiler had been waiting for the doctor, dentist, or real estate broker who shared the communal reception room I would have gotten a business-like nod from Selma. Had she had the place to herself it would have been a grin and, "Long coffee break, Jack."

Mrs. Mannweiler sat ramrod-stiff on a wooden bench against the wall. She was about twenty-five and not attractive. Her nose was too prominent, her mouth too large. When she stood up the baggy brown skirt that was overly long even for her rangy frame showed its need of a pressing. But when she brushed aside a lock of stringy hamster-colored hair and smiled, I decided I liked her.

She followed my lead to a door with *Wellington's National Detective Agency—Louisville Branch* painted in black letters on its frosted glass. It looked impressive even if Louisville was in another state across the river.

After getting her settled in a chair beside my desk, I sat down myself and uncapped a pen. "Is that Mannweiler with one *n* or two?"

"Two. The first name is Margaret but people call me Maggie."

The nickname fit her best. I jotted all of them on a legal pad. When I looked up our eyes met and held a moment, then she leaned closer and said, "I want you to find my father."

I waited, so she relaxed in her chair again. "He's been missing three days."

"You've notified the police?"

"My stepmother has."

I laid the pen on the desk. "The police are better equipped to find him."

She shook her head impatiently. "But they have no reason to. He hasn't committed a crime and he isn't a prominent person."

I smiled, but not much. She had the situation pretty well in focus so I said, "Granted they won't drop the rapes and murders, but they'll do what they can. What's your father's name and what does he do?"

"Raymond Leeth – that's double E. He's an engineer at VTA Electronics."

"It doesn't ring bells."

"VTA is a small plant just off the interstate near Sellersburg. They make computer components. My father's been there since it started in business seven years ago."

"What's VTA stand for?"

"Vaughn Thresher and Associates."

"Your father's an associate?"

"No, he's an employee. Associates are stockholders."

I made a note of the names, then leaned back and said, "So what's it all about?"

She chewed her lower lip, frowning, then took a deep breath. "He left home Saturday morning – this is what my stepmother says – and no one has seen him since. He's never done anything like this before."

"When was the last time you saw him yourself?"

"We had lunch together a week ago today.."

"Did he seem worried or different in any way?"

"Not a bit."

"Think back to your parting. Was it unusual, was there any indication you might not see each other again?"

She shook her head. "Then you think he was planning to disappear?"

I smiled, trying to make it reassuring. "I haven't gotten around to thinking anything yet. You don't live with him and your stepmother?"

"I have my own apartment." She hesitated, then added, "I'm separated from my husband."

"Does he live in town?"

"Yes. Well, not Jeffersonville. Across the river in Louisville."

I studied her features a moment. Each in itself was nothing to boast about but together they made an interesting composite. Her brown eyes continued flecks of green, and a bit of twinkle when she realized she was under scrutiny.

I cleared my throat and said, "When you mentioned your stepmother you seemed doubtful about her."

She gnawed her lip again. "It isn't that I doubt her word. It's just that I never know how certain she is about anything because she drinks too much." She blinked her eyes, then laughed quietly. "I hate it when I get euphemistic. What I meant was, Katie's an alcoholic."

"How long has she been married to your father?"

"A little more than seven years."

"Have they had trouble?"

"No, they pretty much go their separate ways. I suppose you could call that trouble in itself, though."

I straightened up again, ready to end it. "I'll have to talk to her," I said.

She reached for my pen and notepad. "Of course, I'll write down her address. Mine, too, and two numbers where you can reach me." When she finished writing she opened her purse and said, "How much?"

I grinned at her abruptness. "Two hundred a day. Let's start with that."

"That means I'll have to come back tomorrow."

"Even this job has its compensations."

She looked at me a few seconds, then stood up, blushing a little. My eyes followed her to the door. There was an animal magnetism about her that more than made up for any lack of cosmetic charm.

The house was one I had noticed before because of its unusual square tower that began as an arched entryway, then rose three stories. The tower was no more than ten feet square, crowned by a mansard roof with gabled windows on all four sides and wrought iron trim on top. There was a single window on three sides of the second floor and a pair of tall arched ones facing each direction on the third. The house was red brick with white stone at each corner, a small roofed porch at the right of the front door, a sun room extending from the opposite or west side. It was a striking edifice well over a century old. From the top windows of the tower I was certain you could see the Ohio River several blocks south. A lookout so someone now long-dead could watch the comings and goings of the steamboats. A wrought iron fence enclosed an untended yard. As I opened the gate and walked up the sidewalk a curtain was drawn aside from a window to my left. I pretended not to notice.

The woman who opened the door looked sixty-five but I judged her age to be at least ten years under that. A stained, loose fitting black dress added to the aura of physical and emotional emaciation Katie Leeth projected. Her hair hadn't seen a comb in days and her lifeless gray eyes were set deep in clearly defined skeletal pockets above dark pouches.

I flashed my identification but she didn't bother to look. "I'm Jack Rakich," I told her. "Your stepdaughter hired me to find your husband."

"Maggie hired you?" she said vacantly. "Come inside, then."

The house had a stale, unclean odor. I followed her into a room opening left off the entryway. She motioned toward a chair and when I hesitated said, "Go on, nothing that crawls will get on you."

Her voice had grown more forceful after the surprise of having a visitor wore off. She eased herself into a chair next to a small table holding a bottle of Gilbey's gin and a half-empty glass. I sat in one facing her and said, "Any objection to what I'm doing?"

Her laugh rang hollowly in the musty room. "It doesn't matter one way or another to me."

191

"That bad, is it?"

"Not bad, not good, not anything."

"Maggie seems to think highly of your husband."

"Why not? He's been a good father, I suppose."

"But not a good husband?"

She stared off in space a moment. "An indifferent husband, but I knew that about him before we were married. I can't really blame him, we never pretended to be in love. Sometimes I wonder why we even bothered. To get married, I mean."

"How did you meet?"

"Raymond worked for my father. We went out together sometimes, more for convenience than anything else. Business-related social affairs as often as not. So one day we got married."

She drank from the glass beside her, then laughed harshly. "1 honestly can't remember why, or how the subject even came up. It just happened."

"Was it your first marriage?"

She nodded her head a good five seconds, then took another drink. "I suppose that had something to do with it. I was past forty and had given up hope. Not that I'd ever had much anyway. So Raymond came along and was pleasant and, well . . . "

"Was he a widower?"

"No, divorced before he went to work for father. You know about the plant in Bloomington, don't you?"

I shook my head so she said, "Father owned an electronics plant and Raymond was one of his engineers. Not a very good one, though, if you want the truth. More of a librarian, I'd call him. He kept track of things for the *real* engineers."

"Why did he leave?"

"Because there was nothing to stay for; the plant went under a few months after we married. The chief engineer, Vaughn Thresher, had left a short time before to start his own business down here. He took Raymond on, God knows why. Maybe he needed a librarian."

I waited until she emptied her glass, then said, "I didn't think electronic plants went broke these days. What happened?"

She picked up the bottle and held it toward me. "I'm. forgetting my manners, care for a drink?"

Raw gin can make for a short happy hour but I said, "A small one," so she went to another room, came back with a second glass and poured three fingers for me. I swallowed a little of it, then repeated the question about her father's business.

She stared off in space again, lips pursed, then turned to me, both palms upward. "Who knows what happened? Father told me it was piracy, somebody stealing his secrets. They had been developing some new concept or new method of manufacturing, I never did understand the technical points. Whatever, without it the plant wasn't competitive. The business was about to go under, so one night father went home and shot himself."

Her voice had remained steady but there were tears on her cheeks. I decided it was time to switch the conversation back to the present. "You have no idea why your husband left or where he went?"

She dabbed at her cheeks with the end of a ruffled sleeve. "I don't know where he's gone, but I think he left because his scheme had turned sour."

"What scheme was that?"

"I'm not sure what it was, but he had one." She stood up and walked to the center hall, motioning for me to follow. When we reached a room that appeared to be a man's study she went to an old roll-top desk and pulled out a drawer.

"Raymond always kept his desk locked," she said. "He'd have a fit if I even went near it, but after he pulled his disappearing act I decided it was time to see what was so important he had to keep it under lock and key."

I could see where she had jimmied the lock, probably with a screwdriver. She took a bank passbook from a stack of papers in the drawer and handed it to me. "Here, take a look at this."

I pulled the book from its plastic sleeve, flipped pages to the last entry, then whistled softly. "Eighty-one thousand dollars. You didn't know about this?"

"Never even a hint."

"It's a lot of money to keep in a savings account at low interest." I turned back to the front of the book and began reading entries page by page. There had been no withdrawals.

"Regular as clockwork," I said, "a thousand dollar deposit every month for eighty-one months. This was over and above his salary at VTA Electronics?"

"A thousand dollars a month over it."

I compared recent dates in the book with a plastic calendar in my wallet. "Another deposit was due Monday. It's too consistent to be gambling winnings and too much for you to be unaware of unless he was making a lot more money than you knew about. That happens sometimes."

She made a scornful sound. "Raymond didn't earn it."

I tapped the bankbook against the desk for a moment, wondering why Raymond Leeth would leave it behind if he planned to disappear. I said, "Mind if I look around a while?"

Katie Leeth shrugged, no longer interested. She walked out of the room, leaving me alone.

The desk was a labyrinth of cubbyholes and deep drawers with a secret compartment or two probably hidden somewhere. A thorough reading of every document would have taken days and even a cursory search required two hours. The only thing that aroused my curiosity was a phone bill for a Louisville address in the name R. Leath. A billing error, possibly, but it didn't seem likely because a different phone company operated across the river in Kentucky.

Darkness was settling in, my stomach told me the supper hour had come and gone. I slipped the phone bill in my pocket and walked back to the front of the house.

Katie Leeth was alone in the dusky living room, the bottle of gin beside her. "I'm leaving now," I told her. She didn't reply or even bother to look up.

I thought about Raymond Leeth over pizza and chianti at an Italian restaurant on Market across from the shipyard. I could see why he might have decided to chuck it all and start over as Bill Jones in San Diego. I couldn't see why he would leave $81,000 behind. A few visions of what I'd do with that kind of money came to mind. I settled on drifting down the Ohio, then the Mississippi, feet propped on the railing of a small houseboat.

By day the block-long City-County Building was an imposing structure. After dark I always found it somber and oppressive, probably because only the two police stations were open for business. I parked close to the justice wing that formed the shorter portion of an L, then entered double doors facing the

Jeffersonville and Clark County police departments. At the first a detective checked a report, shrugged and said, "Nothing." The answer was the same next door.

"What kind of car does he drive?"

"An eighty-three New Yorker. Deep red."

I thought about crossing the river to Louisville, but instead settled for dialing the number on the phone bill in my pocket. No one answered, so I headed for my apartment.

It was raining when I pushed a curtain aside and looked out on a gray dawn. I brewed coffee, popped a couple of pieces of bread in the toaster, read the morning paper, shaved and showered. The rain had stopped by the time I started out but low gray clouds remained behind. The Sunny Side of Louisville wasn't living up to its name.

After leaving Interstate 65 at the Sellersburg exit I drove west a short distance to a blue prefabricated building that was VTA Electronics. One story of characterless sheet metal, little different than dozens of others close to the interstates in the metropolitan area. Even the receptionist who turned on a corporate smile when I walked in looked like she came with the package.

Getting in to see Vaughn Thresher was almost too easy. I wondered if all unannounced visitors were handed a cup of coffee, then ushered into his private office with time for only a couple of quick gulps. Down-home Hoosier informality seemed a little incongruous in a high-tech setting.

The old-buddy atmosphere apparently originated with Thresher because he was coming around his desk, hand outstretched, when I walked in. He was a beefy character with shirtsleeves rolled twice, sparse hair plastered close to his scalp, a complexion that was too ruddy for his own good. The kind who could have cost me money in a bar because I would have bet he was a salesman, not an engineer or corporate president.

Thresher gave me a hand-on escort to a chair that was functional and lacking warmth like everything else in the office. When he was settled behind his glass and metal desk again he said, "Maggie called the first thing to say you probably would be stopping by. Incomprehensible, this business about her dad."

"I guess that means you have no idea why Raymond Leeth might want to disappear?"

195

"None whatsoever. Ray was the last person on earth I would have pegged for a thing like that. I had very bad vibes about it right from the start."

Very bad vibes moved up right behind *at this point in time* on my hate list after politicians quite using *viable*. I played along, though, and asked, "Why in particular are your vibes bad?"

Thresher pursed his lips and formed a tent with his fingers. "Well, for one thing Ray was a very conservative person in most respects. And very much a creature of habit."

"In what respect wasn't he conservative?" I was also playing along with Thresher's use of the past tense.

"I wouldn't say this under any other circumstances, understand, but hearing about some of the places he was seen hanging out always bothered me. Not so much the riverfront taverns, but" – he paused to giggle self-consciously – "but bars where you find young men and sexual preference might be in question."

"Gay bars, you mean. Are you saying Leeth was a chicken-hawk?"

"Oh, no, don't get me wrong. I just heard things, understand, but you can't help wonder, know what I mean? I just hope he didn't take the wrong person home with him."

"Home with him? He took men home with him?"

Thresher's laugh was forced. "Poor choice of words. I didn't mean *home* literally, know what I mean?"

I thought I probably did. "How long have you known Leeth?" I asked, switching the tense back to present.

"Ten, eleven years. Ray and I worked together at a plant in Bloomington before I started this place. His wife's father owned it, matter of fact."

"From what you said before it must have come as a surprise when he married the boss's daughter."

"Not a bit. Ray Leeth may not have been the best engineer in the world and he may have had some questionable habits, but no one could say he didn't know how to feather his own nest. It didn't work out, of course; her father's business went under."

"Why was that?" I asked, pretending I didn't know.

"Outmoded ideas. The old man was set in his ways; you know how they get so no one can tell them anything. The company fell

196

behind, couldn't compete in today's world."

"But you left before that happened?"

Thresher had a problem letting go of old cliches when new ones came along. He said, "Right. I could see the handwriting on the wall and bailed out. Came down here and set up shop for myself."

"And hired Raymond Leeth. Why, if he wasn't a good engineer?"

The question caught Thresher off guard but you wouldn't have known it if you missed his few quick blinks. "Guess I felt a little sorry for him. Katie, too. But don't get me wrong about Ray. He wasn't what you would call a creative thinker, but what he did, he did well."

"His wife calls him a librarian."

Thresher laughed tersely. "Katie was never one to mince words. Maybe that summed him up, but remember a place like this needs a good librarian, or whatever you want to call it, to operate efficiently."

I edged forward on my chair and said, "Mind if I take a look around the plant?"

"Not at all. Go wherever you like; we're very informal around here. Pride ourselves on that."

I wandered aimlessly a while, thinking the production area didn't look too busy but reminding myself I knew nothing about such operations. Probably all automated so a few people could do the work of a hundred not too many years before.

The offices were laid out in a long row toward the front of the building and seemed busier. I paused to look through a glass door under a sign that read *Engineering*. People were working at tilt tables and I wondered which was Raymond Leeth's, or if he even had one. I turned to go, then stopped when a tall, round-shouldered man carrying several rolled charts came out of an anteroom.

It was the man who had exchanged a large brown envelope for a smaller white one at the diner the previous afternoon. I smiled wryly. It looked like VTA was priding itself on the wrong thing.

Rain began falling again as I drove south on back roads that would take me to Spring Street. 1 found a place to park, then sat a few minutes contemplating the old two-story brick buildings along Jeffersonville's main thoroughfare, wishing it would stop raining and wondering why I hadn't brought a raincoat.

I finally made a run for it and wasn't more than half soaked when I started up the stairs to the office. Several people sat thumbing ragged magazines in the reception area. A shake of Velma's head told me none wanted to see me. After drying off a little I skimmed over a thick packet of material from the home office, then dialed the number of a business writer for one of the Louisville newspapers, a man who owed me a favor or two.

He told me the word going around was that VTA was in trouble. Rumor had it that industrial espionage was the core of the problem. From what he said it was a bigger thing than I had realized, especially in the electronic field. He gave me a little background on Vaughn Thresher – the usual PR stuff – but had never heard of Raymond Leeth.

Next I rang one of the numbers Maggie Mannweiler had left me. When she answered I said, "How about coffee?" She said okay so I named the cafeteria across the street.

Maggie was breathless when she sat down at a table I had picked as far from the other late-morning coffee drinkers as possible. She wiped the water from her face with a paper napkin, then tugged at the wet sleeves clinging to her arms.

"On a day like this you should carry a raincoat," I told her.

She looked around. "Where's yours?"

"I just had to cross the street. There's nothing much to report, but I have a couple of questions. What do you know about industrial espionage? It seems to follow your father around."

She drew herself up, bristling. "Are you implying he's some sort of spy?"

"I'm asking, not implying. It put the plant in Bloomington out of business and now VTA's having the same problem."

Her grip on the edge of the table was so tight her knuckles stood out like eight white knobs. "And you think my father is involved?"

"Say he had a lot of money that couldn't be traced to an explainable source. Any idea where he might have gotten it?"

"Is there a lot of money?"

"Look, we're sitting here asking each other questions but you're not getting paid for it. How about some answers?"

She relaxed her hold on the table and leaned back, the spirit draining from her. "No, I have no idea where it came from or if it even exists. Dad's always been good to me, but not communicative. I know very little about his professional life, but he's a loner, a very private person. I can't picture him being involved in anything that complex."

We drank coffee without saying more for a while, then I said, "I've got another question, and try not to take this one the wrong way. Were there other women in his life?"

She gave me a look of disbelief, then put her head back and laughed. "Glad I'm so entertaining," I told her, so she stopped laughing and leaned toward me, saying, "Why on earth would you ask me that? Surely you can't believe a man would brag about his conquests to his own daughter."

"Okay, then, here's the capper. How about other men in his life?"

It took her a minute to comprehend what I meant, then her cheeks grew fiery. "No," she whispered. After a long pause she said, louder than before, "I'm not trying to be uncooperative, I just don't have the answers to the questions you're asking. How much do most daughters know about their father's private life? Dad and I have been close enough, I think, but that doesn't mean we've shared intimacies."

"Isn't that the way it usually is between parent and child? Isn't it a two-way street of trying to appear better than we are to those close to us?"

She set her cup down, staring across the table at me a moment. Then she said, "You don't impress me as a man who's ever been close to many people."

I crumpled a half-smoked cigarette in the ashtray. "Sometime I'll tell you the story of my life, but right now you're not paying me to hand out any more dime-store philosophy. I have something to check out in Louisville, then I'll get back to you."

The rain had stopped again, the low overcast giving way to patchy clouds and a wind that stirred the water under the Clark Bridge. A tug pushing four barges toward Cincinnati or Pittsburgh hooted from below. As usual, the illusion that the troubles found on shore don't follow you up and down the river gave me some sort of melancholy satisfaction.

The address I wanted turned out to be a three-story apartment on a comer a couple of miles south of the downtown Galleria. It was an old building of buff brick, well cared for and having an air of permanence and stability in a neighborhood of large homes converted to multi-family use half a century earlier.

I ran a finger along a bank of carefully polished brass mailboxes inside the vestibule. When I came to R. Leath I pushed the button beside it a few times without getting a response. The latch hadn't caught on the inner door so I walked inside and on up the stairs to the top floor, then along a wide hallway past doors unable to completely muffle the sound of television sets on the other side.

I knocked lightly at the last apartment on the lop floor, but again without result. A sharp-edged credit card had the door open in seconds. As it swung aside the odor that rushed to meet me made me think I had found Raymond Leeth, however he spelled it south of the Ohio.

I kicked the door shut behind me, breathing through my mouth, reminding myself that I only played a role and somebody else wrote the script.

The body lay on its side at one corner of the kitchen, knees drawn up, left hand clutched against its chest. The right one gripped a knife handle snapped from its blade. The deadly half was imbedded in the chest of the man I recognized from the photograph Maggie had given me.

I looked around the room until I came to a wooden rack with slots for five knives. Four were in place, each with a handle matching the one in Leeth's right hand. A spur-of-the-moment murder, I decided, with the killer making use of the handiest weapon.

The first phone call I didn't mind, the one to the homicide unit downtown. But if there had been a way to avoid calling Maggie Mannweiler I would have jumped at it.

The boys from homicide arrived about the time I was finishing my second cigarette in a chair facing the open door to the outside hall. Bailey, the first one in, went out of his way to play the big dumb cop. It was just an act that sometimes made his job easier;

he was as sharp a detective as you'd find west of the Alleghenies.

He turned to the smaller man behind him. "Jacot, say hello to our friend, the Hoosier shamus." To me he said, "What, you're getting in the habit of bringing your bodies this side of the river and dumping them?"

I gave him a half-hearted smile, then nodded over one shoulder toward the kitchen. "The body's in there. Raymond Leeth, an engineer at VTA Electronics over on the other side. He pulled a Judge Crater four days ago."

"My nose already told me. Where do you fit in?"

"His daughter hired me to find him."

"And—?"

I grinned at him. "Indiana law says I *may* tell you, it doesn't say I *shall* tell you."

"They're speeding a fortune fixing up this neighborhood but to you it still looks like Indiana. Now give."

So I gave him everything I had except a couple of suspicions. Halfway through my spiel Jacot came back from the kitchen to greet the lab crew. When I finished, Bailey said:

"I see it this guy's up to his eyeballs in industrial espionage so somebody decides to put a stop to it. Somebody like your friend Vaughn Thresher. I'm gonna have the county police over there set it up to talk to him."

While Bailey used the phone I walked out in the hall for some air that was a little fresher. From a window overlooking an alley I could see a red New Yorker in a parking stall. After a couple of minutes Bailey bellowed, "Rakich!" I went back inside and found him standing in the center of the living room, hands on hips.

"Would you believe they got their own murder over there?" he said. "Yeah, I can see you would."

It was more than that, I knew. Something closer to home. I said, "Who?"

"Your boy Thresher has gone and got himself killed. So tell me, just where does *that* leave us?"

Jacot had come back into the room. He said, "Suppose the pirate at VTA knew Leeth was wise so he came here and took care of that. Then Thresher got onto him, and ditto."

Bailey started to say something but I got in first with, "Where and how was Thresher killed?"

"Gunned down," Bailey said, "as he was going in a private door at the side of his factory on the way back from lunch. The killer was lying in wait outside, but he gets no sharpshooter's badge. Six shots— probably emptied a revolver—and one hits Thresher. Five scattered around the doorway but the other got him where it hurt most."

I said, "Say Jacot's right, I might have an idea. I'll check it out and let you know."

Bailey turned a bearish scowl my way. "You're going back over? Give us a name first."

"I don't have one. When I do, you'll be the first to know."

Bailey said, "I have bad vibes about this."

I laughed on the way out the door. "We'll be waiting," Bailey called after me.

My call was put through to him an hour later. "That name, it's Daniel Routh. But you don't want him. Let the Clark County police pick him up for peddling plant secrets if they feel like it. That's all he did."

Bailey growled into the phone.

"I checked him out," I told Bailey. "He was in St. Louis from Friday afternoon until Sunday night. It's confirmed, and he was having lunch with three people when Thresher was shot."

"So that leaves us up a stump, right?"

"No, you called it on the nose the first time. Thresher killed Leeth. Leeth knew he was the one who stole secrets at the plant in Bloomington, then used them to open his own place down here. So Leeth collected ever since – first a job, then a thousand under the table every month.

"But then Thresher fell victim to his own game. He was going broke fast, thanks to piracy. He didn't have the cash to go on paying Leeth, and on top of that he suspected Leeth himself was the pirate. So he talked to him Saturday morning, but Leeth wouldn't let him off the hook. They argued back and forth, then Thresher grabbed a knife and ended it the only other way he could think of."

Bailey made a clucking sound with his tongue a while. There was an edge to his voice when he said, "So just going on your hunch we're supposed to wrap this up saying a dead man's the killer? That'll go over great."

"Look, you were right about it from the start. I'm sending a kid over with a photo of Thresher and when you show it around I'll bet you find he was a regular Saturday visitor at the apartment. I'll also bet he was the only one who knew about Leeth's hideaway, the place he went to forget his troubles every chance he got."

Bailey wasn't happy, but there wasn't much he could do about it.

I was starting up the steps when Katie Leeth opened the front door of her house. She looked more relaxed, even smiled a little. "I've been waiting for you," she said.

"You know about your husband?"

"It was on the radio a while ago."

I waited until I was in the same chair again and she was in hers, but without a bottle alongside this time. Then I said, "You killed Vaughn Thresher, didn't you? You finally put it together from the dates in that bankbook."

She smiled again. "You did it for me. I knew Raymond hadn't come by the money honestly, but I hadn't paid enough attention until you spelled it out. Then it was all clear as could be – the reason Vaughn gave him the job, everything."

She paused, shaking her head and still halfway smiling. "Strange, isn't it? All these years and it never once occurred to me that Vaughn had been the one. He and father were always so close, that's what I don't understand. And the ideas he stole, why they really were his own."

"When you shot Thresher you didn't know he had killed your husband, did you?"

She shook her head absently. "Did he?" she said, but without interest. "You know it pushed father into bankruptcy. He put so much of himself into that plant, and then to be betrayed by his most trusted employee. More than an employee, he thought Vaughn was his friend. It killed father, did I tell you that?"

There were tears on her cheeks again. She brushed them aside, pulled out a drawer from the table next to her, removed an old six-shot revolver and handed it to me, saying, "Would you be kind enough to call the police and explain?"

Maggie had been crying, too, when I found her waiting outside the office. Later, after filling in the gaps for her, I said, "You owe the agency for another half a day's work but I'm not going to make an issue of it."

She dabbed at her eyes with a tissue, then gave me her surprised look and something that was midway between a laugh and a sob. "You surely didn't expect me to argue the point, did you?"

"I wouldn't blame you. There hasn't been any good news to report."

"Is that what you normally do, guarantee a happy ending?"

I smiled at her. It was no prize winner, but she gave me one of her own. Then she sank back in her chair, wrinkling her brow and sighing. "It's going to be difficult thinking of dad as a blackmailer."

"Don't, then," I told her. "Don't moralize. He was under terrific pressure seven years ago. Out of a job, a teenage daughter to get through school, a wife devastated by the loss of her own father.

"But I think what bothered him more than anything else was knowing he wasn't respected as an engineer. He could see only one way out, take advantage of what he knew about Vaughn Thresher. Then when it worked and he had a job again, he decided to go one step further. You'll never know why – he may not have himself – but try to take into account the strain he had been under. The strange thing is, or maybe it isn't, he never spent a penny of the money he didn't earn."

She sat quietly a moment, then opened her purse. "I'll write you a check now." She stood up as she handed it to me, smiling as best she could. "Thanks, I do appreciate what you've done."

I locked the office behind us and followed her down the stairs. On the sidewalk she turned with another halfway smile, then walked south to a rusty little Toyota. As she bent to unlock the door I called, "Maggie."

Her head turned and I said, "Unless you have other plans, how about a drink and something to eat?"

She smiled – a broad one this time – and hurried back along the sidewalk.

ALSO AVAILABLE BY DICK STODGHILL

Volume 1, Jack Eddy Stories
The first eight stories in the popular series featuring private eye Jack Eddy and his reporter friend Bram Geary set in Akron, Ohio, circa 1937. .

Midland Murders
Seven stories from Alfred Hitchcock's Mystery Magazine and one from Ellery Queen's Mystery Magazine. Included is the complete Hal Blinn-Grady Driscoll series.

From Devout Catholic to Communist Agitator – The Helen Lynch Story
A true story that for decades left people wondering why this young woman suddenly cut all ties with her family and later became an active leader of the Communist Party.

Normandy 1944 – A Young Rifleman's War
Neither sanitized nor glamorized, this is the story of a young World War II soldier as seen from ground level. Acclaimed as an outstanding account of the horrors of combat.

These books are available from Amazon, Barnes & Noble and other online sites or may be ordered from any bookstore if not in stock.   Visit: www.dickstodghill.com

www.ingramcontent.com/pod-product-compliance
Lightning Source LLC
Chambersburg PA
CBHW020421180626
46812CB00003B/1082